TAKEN

LISA MARIE RICE

Published by Oliver Heber Books

Copyright 2022 Lisa Marie Rice

Cover Design by Sweet 'N Spicy Designs

978-1-648-39-351

&. Created with Vellum

PUBLISHER'S NOTE: This is a work of fiction. Names, characters, places, and incidents either are the product of the author's imagination or are used fictitiously. Any resemblance to actual persons, living or dead, business establishments, events, or locales is entirely coincidental.

Published by Oliver-Heber Books

Taken © 2022 Lisa Marie Rice

Cover Design by Sweet 'N Spicy Designs

0 9 8 7 6 5 4 3 2 1

 Created with Vellum

1

Give me your daughter.

Marcus Rey thought the words but didn't say them. He'd have her soon enough.

Lightning crackled outside the huge French windows, lighting the room with phosphorescent light. Harrington Banner's study was kept deliberately dark, with only two banker's lamps on. But the sudden intense lightning showed what Banner was trying to hide.

The study was diminished from its former glory. It was shabby and dusty. Several paintings were missing —lighter spots on the wall. Harrington Banner's family had collected art, had been known for their possession of a few grand masters, and for possessing ten Picassos, two Renoirs and four Jackson Pollacks.

The missing paintings had been large, big white rectangles in dirty cream walls. Banner had probably sold a few Pollacks, hoping to make a dent in his debts.

He hadn't. Banner still owed a fuck-ton of money to some very bad people. And now, since this morning, Banner owed that money to him.

Lightning bloomed again, followed by a violent

crack of thunder. Marcus let his gaze roam thought-fully around Banner's once-elegant study. He had ex-cellent night vision. Chipped Georgian furniture, a stained Aubusson carpet. A Chippendale desk that needed restoring. Empty shelves where first editions had been auctioned off.

Another year of this, and the house itself would be the next to go. Maybe sooner. Harrington Banner was one of those men who were slaves to their appetites. He had three expensive mistresses, his golf club fees were over a hundred grand per annum, he ran tabs at most of the expensive restaurants in the city. Marcus also wondered whether Banner had a cocaine habit.

Probably.

Not much was coming in, either. Harrington Banner IV had an aversion to work. He didn't mind showing up in his fancy expensive office downtown, but once he was there, from what Marcus could see by hacking into his firm's ridiculously lax accounts, Banner did fuck-all. He lost money for himself and for his clients and it had been over a year since he'd had a new client.

His golf handicap was great, though.

He'd inherited a fortune and had fucked it almost all away. Right now, Banner was a whisper away from total ruin. Marcus would have happily tipped him over, except Banner had something Marcus wanted.

Badly.

Marcus had nothing but contempt for the man. Marcus had raised himself up from the streets by smarts and by iron self-control. Banner had had the world handed to him and had pissed everything away. Including a wife and child, dumping them cruelly. It was only because of his daughter's generosity of spirit that she was still speaking to him.

Lightning lit up the room again, like a strobe effect, followed a second later by a loud boom. And another. Rain lashed the windows, making them rattle. The storm was right overhead, as powerful as a war.

Banner started at the boom, perspiration at his hairline. At some animal level, Banner realized that nature was powerful, and not impressed by wealth or power. Certainly not fading wealth and obsolete power.

Marcus hadn't started at the violent sound. Violence was a part of his life, had been forever. He was never surprised. Surprise had been beaten out of him on the streets at a very young age. He didn't do surprise. Or fear.

"So." Banner tried to infuse impatience into his voice, but it wavered. "How can I help you, Mr.— ahem... I'm sorry, I didn't catch your name."

Marcus almost smiled. Banner knew his name. Everyone knew his name, though no one knew *him*. His name was never in the newspapers. He never attended parties and was never seen around town. And yet everyone knew about him. He was immensely rich though no one really knew where the money had come from. But money had its own gravity and weight.

"Marcus Rey," he said softly. "My name is Marcus Rey. And what do I want? I want your daughter."

Banner jumped in his luxurious leather chair. His eyes rounded. For a second, his mask of bored rich man slipped and he looked panicky. "I-I beg your pardon?"

"You heard me." Marcus's voice was low and soft but Banner jumped again, as if he'd shouted.

"This is insane." Banner placed two soft white hands on his desk, preparing to stand, though he looked like he wanted to puke. "I'm afraid I'm not in the mood for jokes in very poor taste. I'll have to ask you to--"

"I bought your debt to Hector Lopez. It's mine, and now you owe the money to me. I think you know owing money to Lopez is ill-advised. Frightening. But I assure you, Mr. Banner, owing money to *me* is terrifying."

He let the words hover there in the air in the dark study. He knew enough about weak men to know that what was going on in Banner's mind was more frightening than anything he could say. Most of the rumors about Marcus were wrong, but not all of them. Banner *should* be terrified of him.

Except for the fact that he had the one thing Marcus wanted. Very badly.

Marcus leaned forward, his voice still soft, but he was certain Banner heard every single word. "There is no way you can repay that debt, certainly not by next week, which is when it comes due. And not by next year. You'd have to sell this—" Marcus waved his hand to indicate the study and its contents, but also Waverly Mansion, which had been in Banner's family for four generations.

Though the grounds weren't kept well and it was falling into shabbiness, it was still beautiful, like a former beauty queen who'd aged badly, but still had good bones. "You could liquidate all your holdings, and it wouldn't be enough, not in today's market. I could make you throw in Waverly Mansion to pay off your debt to me."

Sweat was coming off of Banner in rivulets. He exuded fear sweat, a sickening smell mixed with his Hugo Boss cologne. Every word Marcus said was true, and they both knew it. And they both knew Banner didn't have the money, didn't have close to the amount needed to pay his debts. Right now, he was living off 'loans' from his daughter.

"What—what is it you said you wanted?" Banner's voice quavered, his hands trembled. Marcus had grown up learning the hard way never to show any kind of emotion, most of all fear. Never *ever* show fear. But Banner had never been in a position where he had no escape.

He owed a lot of money to Lopez first, and now to him. He didn't have it and had no way to earn it. He was like a rat caught in a trap.

"Your daughter," Marcus said, his voice hard.

Banner winced. But he didn't say no.

The fucker.

Marcus felt pure contempt for the man. If Marcus had a daughter and someone had just made an offer to buy her, he'd have slashed the man's throat the instant the words were out of his mouth.

Banner knew Marcus as a dangerous man. Marcus had carefully cultivated his reputation as a dangerous man. Marcus would rather tear his own throat out than harm Banner's daughter in any way, but Banner didn't know that.

"Your daughter will be here soon. She visits you every Thursday. When she arrives, you will introduce me to her as a close friend of yours. A man she can trust." Banner winced again. But again, he didn't say no. "If you are convincing, I will wipe out your debt."

Banner blinked and Marcus suppressed a smile.

"And one further thing, Banner. You will not ask her for a loan. You will never ask her for money again. Ever. You already owe her $250,000 you have no intention of paying back, and she is struggling to pay her mortgage. So all that sponging off your daughter is over."

Marcus knew his face was a mask and didn't show his rage and disgust. Banner was perfectly willing to sponge off his daughter who had made every penny she had through hard work. Marcus also knew his own face was cold and implacable.

"I know everything about you. How your second wife has filed for divorce and has a really good lawyer. She is aiming to drain every penny from your bank account, though she doesn't know there's nothing there. I know that you left your first wife and hired a vicious attorney to make sure she got a bad settlement. And when your first wife developed cancer, you used that to cut her completely off because you knew she and your daughter were too busy fighting the disease to file an appeal. Your daughter nearly killed herself working three jobs to put herself through college and pay off the medical bills. But now, with her podcasts, she's earning decent money and you 'reconnected'. And starting asking for loans immediately."

Banner glanced at him then looked away, as if completely incapable of looking at him for any length of time. But, then, Banner's life hadn't given him much need to stare unfavorable facts, or hostile gazes, in the face.

Marcus let the silence build up. He'd stated what he wanted. Now Banner had to give it to him.

"I can't—I can't just 'give' my daughter to you. What do you want with her?"

"Sex," Marcus answered.

Banner flinched, a drop of sweat flung onto the desk.

"Pops?" A soft voice from the doorway.

There she was. Eve Banner, the creator of the hit podcast *Banner's Books*. She walked in, carrying the essence of springtime into the dark winter afternoon.

Marcus rose from his chair out of deference to a lady, but also because he knew from experience that if he stood up to his full height while she was close to him, she would feel overpowered. If he stood while she walked toward him, she would have time to adjust. Feel less crowded.

His size and obvious strength intimidated a lot of people and he used that fact often. There were plenty of people in this world he wanted to intimidate, to frighten, but not Eve. Never Eve.

Marcus eyed her hungrily as she crossed the room, grace in every line of her slender body. This was the closest he'd ever been to her and every step she took seemed to echo in every beat of his heart.

He never missed her podcasts, streaming the shows on *YouTube* over and over again until he knew the programs by heart. He attended all of her in-person shows. She'd given a show two weeks ago on new mystery authors and he'd stood at the back of the packed hall and watched her. Watched her charming the crowd with her gentle humor, touching their hearts with her understanding of human nature. Treating her guests with great respect so that the discussion was easy-going, bringing out the best of each guest, even the introverts.

Twice he'd sat in his car outside her bedroom window, waiting for the odd glimpse before she shuttered her windows for the night. He stopped that. It was insane behavior. He was compelled by forces he couldn't comprehend, but that were massively strong.

This was the first time he'd been within touching distance. He could feel his heartbeat in his chest, in his fingertips, in his cock.

He'd seen her first on a TV program. One dark, rainy night after defeating a vicious takeover attempt, when he'd felt despair seep into his soul, he downed half a bottle of Glenfiddich, remaining stone cold sober.

Reading had helped for a while, as it always did. It had staved off the loneliness and heartsickness, but the book had ended, as did everything.

Deep in the Beast. He could have sworn the author had had a direct line into his soul. He'd turned the book over and studied the author's picture. Lamont Serrin. A young black man with dreadlocks and small, scholar's glasses perched on his nose. Dark, piercing, all-seeing eyes and a poet's mouth.

It was as if Serrin had spoken for Marcus, had lived Marcus's childhood and written about it. The shock of reading his deepest thoughts was still echoing when Marcus turned on his TV and stopped, frozen. It was Lamont Serrin, talking. But what had him springing to his feet to come closer to the wall-sized screen was the woman Serrin was talking to.

Beautiful, yes, but then most women on TV were good-looking. Good skin, good teeth, styled hair, elegant clothes. A ton of people in the background working to make them look good. It went with the territory. Women on media could buy whatever elements of attraction they wanted.

But this woman had an old-fashioned beauty, a romantic beauty, tinged with sadness. She looked like a time traveler, beamed in from another time and another place, a world where nobody played games. The expression on her heart-shaped face was intent as she spoke with the young black man, speaking somehow to Marcus, too. It was as if she could read *his* mind, *his* heart. Understood exactly what that kind of childhood meant.

All his life, Marcus had felt alone. He was used to

it, used to feeling on his own. And in one night, two strangers reached out to him, spoke to his heart. One a beautiful woman. Eve Banner.

He watched her videos religiously after that and made it his business to find out everything about her. Finding things out about people, legally, illegally, was just one of his many money-making talents.

The more he found out about Eve Banner, the more obsessed he became. Through his sources he discovered her history, her likes, her dislikes. Her courage, her steadfastness, her loyalty. Her intelligence, her gentleness.

With a curious look at Marcus, Eve walked up to her father's desk. "You okay, Pops?" she asked, a frown bringing together ash-brown eyebrows.

It wasn't an idle question. Harrington Banner looked like he was about to have a stroke. His hands, clasped on a leather blotter, trembled. Banner looked at Marcus, winced. "Sure, honey. Sure. I'm fine." He tried to smile, showing teeth. "It's good to see you."

Marcus lowered his head, turned and stared coldly at Banner. Angry at the show of fatherly love that was a fucking sham. Banner loved no one but himself. Not his daughter, not his first wife, not his second wife, who was speaking to the most vicious divorce lawyer in the city right now. Charlene Banner was going to go ballistic when she discovered there was nothing left to grab. Even Waverly Mansion would go someday soon.

But it was Banner's treatment of his daughter that enraged Marcus. Banner had left when Eve was ten, and rarely made child support payments. After growing up with wealth, Eve had been plunged into poverty almost overnight. Eight years later, her mother had breast cancer and they discovered they'd been taken off Banner's health insurance.

Eve put herself through college with scholarships and writing book blogs. Then came her wildly successful show, *Banner's Books*. Every single show was exciting, funny and moving.

Though nothing in his life would lead anyone to think it, Marcus loved books. Books saved his life when he was a street rat sleeping rough on the streets. He was in and out of school, but the instant he learned to read, he taught himself everything. He'd hide out in local libraries where the punks would never find him and taught himself economics, history, politics. He understood clearly that knowledge was power. He rose quickly to the top of a criminal empire because he was smart and ruthless but also because he read, and understood how the wider world worked. So–useful tool.

But what he never let anyone find out about himself was that he also read for pleasure—the classics, the genres, poetry. He read widely and secretively and never shared his passion. Never wanted to. Never even thought of it. Until her. Until Eve.

That evening of quiet despair when he happened upon her show–it was like she was channeling him. From then on, he read what she recommended and loved the books. She enchanted him, fascinated him, in a way that had never happened to him before. The way her mind worked, the way she was able to put even difficult guests at ease, what interested her, what bored her. It was all so fascinating. Whenever she did a live show with a live audience, he was there, hidden far in the back.

He knew most things about her life.

He also knew she was single.

That was about to end.

He shot a cold look at Banner, who drew in a sharp breath.

"Honey," Banner said, voice tight. He coughed to ease it, looking stressed.

"Do you have a cold, Pops?" Eve frowned.

"No, no." Banner tried smiling again. "No, not at all. Honey, I'd like to introduce a–a friend of mine, Marcus Rey."

She turned to him, smiling, hand out. "Nice to meet you, Mr. Rey."

Marcus took her hand, careful not to hold it a second longer than he should. Though he wanted to hold on to it forever. Soft skin, long slender fingers, her hand felt wonderful in his. The day would come when he would hold more than her hand, but for now, he simply savored the moment and released her hand.

"Likewise, Dr. Banner. I'm a big fan of your show."

Her smile lit up the room. "Oh really? How kind of you to say so. If you're a friend of my father's, I can leave a ticket for you at my next talk. I've got a TED talk coming up at the Derry Center. Early in January."

He already had a ticket, a seat in the back of the room, but he bowed his head. "I'd be very grateful, thank you."

Banner's heavy breathing broke the silence of the room and Eve turned with a frown. "You sure you're okay, Pops?"

"Fine, fine," he gasped. Well, hell. Marcus would have to go before Banner had a freaking heart attack. The fuck was the matter with him?

Eve turned to him with a smile. "How do you know my father, Mr. Rey?"

Marcus flicked a dark glance at Banner—*keep your fucking mouth shut*—and gave an easy smile. "We had business dealings, Dr. Banner, and we became friends."

"Eve," she said.

"Eve." He bowed his head. "And I'm Marcus."

"Marcus."

She sat down in the other club chair, graceful and composed. Marcus did his best not to stare, but *damn*. She had this quiet kind of beauty it took a while to notice, but Marcus noticed. Oh yeah. He'd noticed right from the start. Sometimes the screen changed looks but she looked just as good without makeup and without lighting as she did on the screen.

Shoulder-length light chestnut hair that seemed to have every color under the sun, even in the dim light of her father's study. Colors from ash blonde to dark red. Unusual light gray eyes with a dark gray rim, surrounded by thick dark eyelashes. Compelling eyes, witch's eyes, that seemed to see more than most people. Small, straight nose, sculpted cheekbones, a sinfully large mouth, perfect pale skin that looked like ivory silk. Graceful. Not tall, but long-limbed.

Some deeply elusive and mysterious scent.

Marcus had to stop himself from leaning in to her to catch more of it. He had to clench his hands to keep from touching that fine smooth skin.

His intense desire was... inexplicable. Marcus had all the sex he wanted. Though not a public figure, he was rich and powerful. Women could sense that, could *smell* that. He'd never had any trouble at all finding women to bed. He never paid for it, but the evenings out at top restaurants, the jewelry, the nights in five-star hotels... it all worked. Sex was a transaction and he was, above all, a businessman. He understood what was happening and so did the women. That kind of sex was all he'd ever wanted. Pleasant evening out, a tumble between the sheets, preferably in an upscale hotel, departing before dawn. A transaction.

But with Eve, he didn't want a transaction, he didn't want just sex in exchange for a diamond bracelet. He wanted sex, but he wanted her company, her conversation, he wanted *her*.

Banner was gasping for air, the moron. He was probably distressed that he couldn't ask Eve for another 'loan'. *Well, fuckhead, those days are forever over*. Banner would know that Marcus would find out immediately if Eve made another deposit in his bank account. Or maybe Banner was just worried about wife number two finding out about his mistresses and doubling her alimony request. Or maybe he was worried that as Waverly Mansion was so run-down, the three real estate agencies he had quietly contacted had given insultingly low quotes.

Whatever. Marcus didn't care. Though he found it actually painful to leave a room Eve was in, his goal had been achieved. Eve knew him as a friend of her father's and therefore harmless. Marcus was anything but harmless, he was ferociously dangerous. But not to her. Never to her.

He knew exactly what he wanted from Eve, but it wasn't to hurt her. It was to give her blinding pleasure.

Later.

He stood. Nodded his head at Banner. "Harrington. A pleasure as always."

Banner nodded his head back, shakily, looking like someone had stunned him with a cattle prod.

"Marcus." His face had been almost plum-colored before, a heart attack in waiting, but now he was deathly pale. Was he about to stroke out?

Whatever Banner's problems, Marcus didn't give a shit. He turned to what he did care about, a lot.

"Eve. It was a pleasure. I hope to see you again." Soon. Soon. *Soon*. There was a drumbeat of anticipation in his head, booming. In his head, he cut through everything—drinks, dinner—straight to an image of Eve naked, in his bed. All that beautiful pale skin, his to touch. Those remarkable witch's eyes, fixed on him as he prepared to mount her... He suppressed a shiver.

Eve eyed her father and stood. Banner looked startled. "You're leaving so soon, darling? I wanted to chat with you. Um, for a while."

Marcus shot him a vicious glance. Fucker was *not* going to ask her for more money. That was fucking over. Banner caught the look and bit his lips.

"Sorry, Pops." Eve bent down and kissed her father's sweat-damp forehead. "I promised I'd teach a class at the Heritage Center. Some really great kids, lots of talent."

Marcus froze. Heritage Center. Shit. That was in a really dangerous part of town. A woman like her, beautiful, well-dressed ... well, she'd be a lamb to the slaughter.

Banner frowned. "The Heritage Center? Darling, that's in a very rough part of town. Do be careful."

Eve sighed. "Yeah, I know. When I accepted, the talk was scheduled at a downtown bookstore, but they shifted the venue and I didn't have the heart to refuse. I'll be fine. I'll take precautions." She checked her watch, eyes widening in dismay, and rose. "And... I'm late! Bye Pops, Marcus, really good meeting you."

Marcus waited until she walked out the door, whirled on Banner and bunched his sweat-soaked linen shirt in his fist. "You were going to ask her for more money, weren't you? You forgot and you were going to ask. You were probably going to ask for cash, so it wouldn't show up in your bank account."

Banner winced, pressed his back against his desk chair, trying to avoid Marcus's grip. But it was unbreakable. Marcus shook Banner like a dog. "I have my eye on you, Banner, and if I see that you have taken another cent from your daughter you will be very sorry. Owing money to Lopez is bad, but owing money to me is worse. I'm much more dangerous to you than he is. Are we clear?" Banner just sat, sweating, open mouthed. Marcus shook him again. "*Are we clear?*"

"C-crystal," he gasped.

Marcus let go of Banner's shirt with an expression of disgust. The man didn't deserve a daughter like Eve. With one last, hard look, he left.

LOW-LIFE ASSHOLE, Harrington Banner thought viciously. Fucking gangster. Before his unfortunate financial setbacks, Banner hadn't had contact with men such as Marcus Rey. Or Hector Lopez. But since he'd lost a considerable amount of money in a market downturn, totally not his fault, he'd had many dealings with the species and every time, he felt like he should take a long hot shower to get the stench of the street off him.

He hadn't actually met Marcus Rey before. Though he knew the man was rich, he had no idea how he'd made his money. He wasn't as infamous as Lopez, known for his violence. Marcus Rey wasn't known for much beyond his wealth and the mysterious ways he'd made his wealth. But there were whispers that you didn't want to cross him. And now that... that *creature* held him in his grip.

For a moment, Banner shivered. He'd felt that powerful grip, quite literally. A huge, dark hand nearly lifting him out of his chair, the physical power of him palpable. For a man so controlled, he'd looked like he was on the verge of exploding. Face taut with some kind of strong emotion. A vein standing out on his temple, jaws clenched. Shoulders so broad they blocked out Banner's view until all he saw was a huge expanse of dark overcoat and that enormous fist at his throat.

Banner was used to fear ever since some unfortunate investments hollowed him out, but this personal, in-your-face physical fear of someone touching him—someone immensely powerful and unafraid of using that power—was new. It was diminishing.

How dare Marcus threaten him, *touch* him, as if they were equals. Banner might be experiencing a temporary downturn, but that did not give Marcus Rey permission to manhandle him. Banner had never been manhandled in his life, and had no intention of ever allowing it again.

What did he know of Rey? Not much. Nobody knew anything. He'd come up from the streets, made a fortune and basically disappeared from sight, while his reputation and his fortune grew. Shadowy and mysterious, with enemies everywhere.

Particularly Andrei Petrov. Head of the Russian Bratva in the city. Rumor had it that their enmity went back to their childhood, when they were both street rats. They hated each other.

Hmmm.

Andrei Petrov. Another vicious low life. Less mysterious than Rey. Someone who liked to live large and be seen doing it. And unlike Rey, he was involved in drugs. And also unlike Rey, batshit crazy.

Petrov had bought the penthouse in the Carical Building and had, famously, painted it all gold. The bathroom fixtures were gold. There were photos of the penthouse, in appallingly bad taste.

But no one knew where Rey lived. Why was that? Was it because Rey was afraid of Petrov?

What would Petrov pay to have information on Rey? To know of a weakness he had?

It took a while, but he got Petrov's cell number. It would be one of many. These criminals had a plethora of cells, for security reasons. Banner didn't care. All he cared about was to convey something to Petrov, in exchange for money.

When he finally made his way through the many cut-outs and 'assistants', he heard a deep voice come online, pure street in his voice, thick Russian accent. "Yo, whozzis?"

It took Banner a while, but he finally had Petrov's full attention when he mentioned Marcus Rey. He negotiated a price and gave Petrov what he wanted. A weakness.

"Marcus Rey is interested in my daughter," Banner said.

2

"Thanks so much, Dr. Banner. You coming here means a lot to our kids." Eve smiled at Yasmine Hassid, the energetic head of the Youth Program at the Heritage Center. Eve could see she meant every word. And the kids had been incredibly enthusiastic. They'd crowded around the podium, in a cacophony of voices, vying for her attention, keeping her there an extra hour. Of course, Eve's topic, storytelling in comic books, might have had something to do with it.

"My pleasure," Eve answered Yasmine, and meant it. "Let me know the results of the competition."

The Heritage Center was sponsoring a competition for best new superhero and Eve had committed to showcasing the top three on her show in the new year. She was sure she could help facilitate a contract between a young comics publishing company she knew and the three top talents.

She *loved* this. Loved finding new talent, helping them, like planting a seed and watching a flower grow. But she'd stayed much longer than she'd planned. She wanted to finish while there was still daylight but it was dark outside now, as she could see from the windows high up on the walls.

The area was full of good people but they were all safely indoors, now. This was not an area where single women should be out on the streets alone after dark.

Of course, she took precautions. She had pepper spray in her purse, right on top of the contents of the purse, within easy grabbing distance. She always walked close to the walls, away from the street side of the sidewalk. Her car was parked only two blocks away. Five minutes after leaving the Center, she'd be inside her locked car, on her way home.

Still, it would have been nice if someone had been waiting for her, to walk her safely back to her car. To show they cared.

When she'd accepted a two-week volunteer stint at the Moss Foundation in another rough part of town, her father had promised to pick her up after the lectures. She had thought that finally, finally things could go right between them when he said that, but she should have known better.

Her father had recently come back into her life after being absent for almost twenty years. He hadn't even made contact while her mother was dying of breast cancer. Still, he'd made an effort.

After the first lecture, she'd waited over an hour for him to show up until the janitor had had to turn out the lights in the shabby auditorium. The same thing happened at the next lecture. The first time, he'd called up the next morning to apologize and offer some excuse. The second time, he hadn't even bothered to call. The third time, she hadn't waited for him and they never mentioned it again.

In her heart, Eve knew why he'd contacted her again. Because her show *Banner's Books* was a huge success and she earned well. He hadn't hesitated to ask for money and, though she'd hesitated, in the end she gave him what he asked for. She felt contempt for him, when she wanted to feel love. But... he was her only living relative. She tried, she really did, but she had to be content with his superficial charm and elegant manners.

But he was unreliable. He'd never be waiting for her, ever.

Eve blinked. She thought she saw a figure at the back. A big man, dressed in black. A little like... a little like the man she'd met at her father's house. Marcus Rey. She'd heard of him, vaguely. One of those people who mattered but who had nothing to do with her. Still, in person, he made a huge impression. He was a striking man. Austere, harsh, sharp features, very tall, huge shoulders, massively built. But soft spoken and impeccably polite.

Why was she thinking of him when she should be hurrying home? Marcus Rey. Her father knew Marcus Rey. That blew her mind. Her father's friends were other trust fund men, soft and silly, mainly concerned with their expense accounts and golf handicap. Not hard men.

This man was hard, like granite, as mysterious as he was notorious. His name was never in the newspapers. He never attended parties and was never seen around town. And yet everyone knew about him. Though immensely rich, no one really knew where the money came from.

Gun-running, she suspected. Smuggling maybe. Not drugs. The one indisputable fact about Marcus Rey that she knew was that he hated drugs.

He was a man who was beyond the bounds of society, essentially an outlaw. How on earth could her father know such a man? Be friends with him? There were a lot of things she didn't know about her father,

but she would have said a friendship with Marcus Rey
was impossible. Life took such odd turns.

In college, she'd dated a pre-med student whose
mother had been a drug addict. Ed could afford college because he'd been bankrolled by Marcus Rey. It
was the first time she'd ever heard of him. Ed had
mentioned his name in a whisper. When she'd asked
if Ed was afraid of him he'd said no, but that Rey had
enemies everywhere. But in his underground way, he
helped the victims of drug abuse.

That was all she'd ever been able to pry out of Ed
and had only heard the name Marcus Rey spoken a
few times, always in a whisper, until she unexpectedly
came across him in her father's study.

She shivered suddenly at the memory. Ed hadn't
mentioned how tall and big Rey was. How imposing.
How he utterly dominated a room. How power
seemed to emanate from him like an aura.

She started as a bank of lights went out with an
echoing *thunk!* Time to go. Even the janitor was sick of
waiting for her.

Eve started stuffing her briefcase with the comic
books, graphic novels and the laptop with the slide
deck she'd used in the course on comic books. A book
fell off the edge of her desk and the sound echoed
eerily in the empty hall. Another bank of lights shut
down. The janitor was doing her a favor, letting her
pack up. He could just as easily suddenly plunge her
into darkness, which in this neighborhood was
dangerous.

Danger.

Marcus Rey had a reputation as a very dangerous
man to know. Not a man to cross, not a man you'd
want as your enemy. Dark rumors swirled about his
name.

But maybe he wasn't so dangerous, after all, if he was her father's friend.

Very dangerous to women, though, she imagined. Certainly dangerous to *her* peace of mind. She couldn't shake him from her thoughts. She could still see him, in her mind's eye. Short black hair, black eyes, dark blade-like features, black linen jacket, black silk shirt, black fine wool trousers. Big black overcoat, made of some superfine material. Probably cashmere.

He was immense—powerful and dark, with an almost palpable aura of menace around him. He also had seemed superbly fit. For all his size, he had moved with the grace of a panther.

A small sound at the back of the hall made her lift her head suspiciously.

The Heritage Center was in the roughest part of town, sometimes called No Man's Land. Of course, she took precautions, but she was filled with unease.

It would have been nice to have someone waiting for her, to walk her safely back to her car. Someone who cared, someone to watch over her.

In the large, dark auditorium, something shifted in her heart.

Eve's hands stilled at the thoughts running through her head. This was totally unlike her. Since when did she want someone watching over her? She didn't need anyone.

She'd had a lover or two. She dated. Some. Not much, but enough to know that she wasn't missing much by not having a man in her life. She was used to solitude. After her father had abandoned them, she'd watched her mother descend into a frightening depression and then into illness. She'd dealt with it all on her own.

She'd learned early on the price you paid for love

and trust and it had never seemed worthwhile up... up until now. What was this? Why was she even thinking of a man to protect her? She'd been on her own for as long as she could remember and had learned the hard way to look after herself. Not to count on anyone else. Men were weak, anyway.

Most men.

A sudden vision of Marcus Rey, standing silently in her father's study, flashed before her eyes. He hadn't seemed weak at all. He looked exactly like the kind of man who would protect to the death what was his.

Stop that, Eve told herself. She knew nothing about Marcus Rey, except that he had a reputation as a dangerous man. In the rare moments when she had fantasized about falling in love, she'd imagined someone gentle and tender. Certainly not someone like Marcus Rey, a man who walked in darkness.

Her thoughts were hormonal. She'd just met a man who attracted her on a physical level, something that rarely happened. So her hormones were projecting God knows what onto a man she didn't know except by reputation. And that reputation wasn't good.

Oh God. Sandbagged by her own hormones. Such a dangerous thing.

She was the last person in the large auditorium. The janitor, an elderly Black man, waited at a side door. He motioned to her and she waved back. For a moment, Eve thought she saw a large, dark figure behind him and her heart leapt. But there was no one there.

The janitor blacked out the entire auditorium.

For a moment, she thought she'd seen Marcus Rey. Now her hormones were making her see things that weren't there. She shook herself and tried to focus on her surroundings. Maybe once she got home safely and sat in her favorite chair with a cup of tea, she could let herself go and wonder about the man who'd made such a strong impact on her senses. Maybe in bed make use of that vibrator a friend had given her as a joke. Get rid of this tension that was clearly sexual.

But not now. Walking out on these streets while distracted was a pretty good way to commit suicide.

Two women had been attacked in the area in the last month.

Eve kept her cellphone in her coat pocket, switched on, with 911 on speed dial. She kept her car fob in her coat pocket, within easy reach. She had pepper spray right at the top of the contents of her purse. She'd taken a self-defense course. She was as ready as any woman could be.

She walked across the dark auditorium, the sound of her high heels echoing sharply in the large space, rolling her eyes at herself at the sound. Lower heels would have been better, but she'd had so little time to change, she'd forgotten.

Eve pushed open the heavy steel doors of the auditorium and gave a gasp, shrinking back instinctively as a bright bolt of lightning cut through the bruised-looking sky, followed immediately by a clap of thunder so loud she felt as if her eardrums would burst. The rain was coming down so hard it looked more like a waterfall than a shower, pellets of water bouncing waist-high off of the cracked sidewalks. She waited a moment to see if the heavy rain subsided a little. It didn't, so she sighed and set off, holding her briefcase over her head.

Maybe if she'd spent less time in the center mooning over Marcus Rey, she'd be halfway home by now. Skittering in her high heels down the sidewalk, trying to avoid the major puddles, she was soaked within a minute. The roar of the rain was deafening and she could barely see more than a foot ahead of her. At least the weather should keep the low-lifes away. She hoped.

Ducking her head down lower, she tried to pick up speed. Another minute and she'd reach the car...

Eve staggered at the sharp blow to her head. It took her completely by surprise and almost knocked her off her feet. She thudded into the brick wall she'd been following by touch more than by sight. A heavy body slammed into her.

She couldn't catch her breath, her bearings. Wheezing, she tried to pull in air, but it didn't work. Her ears rang and she couldn't focus her eyes.

It was all so sudden, she didn't have a chance to react. Men with sharp, angry faces surrounded her. She blinked blood out of her eyes as one of the men tore her purse out of her hands. He opened it, looking inside. With a laugh, he tossed out the pepper spray. Instinctively, Eve reached for the spray bouncing away and received another hard slap which made her head bounce off the wall and her vision black out for a second.

One of the men grabbed her coat, spinning her around.

Fumbling, fingers numb, she tried to get to the cellphone in her coat pocket, but her fingers tangled with his and he pulled it out and threw it to the ground.

Dazed, Eve stared at the plastic rectangle in a puddle of muddy water. Salvation, out of reach. Whimpering, she stretched her hand down towards the phone and received a powerful punch to the stomach that flung her against the wall. The pain was blinding, crackling all through her body. It hurt to breathe. She tried to push herself off from the wall but one of the men body-blocked her.

She sagged weakly. The man's body tightly pressed against hers was the only thing holding her upright. She tried to pull away from him, but there was only the hard brick wall against her back.

"Who the fuck ya callin', huh?" the man breathed into her ear. His breath was horrid—hot and fetid with the smell of alcohol, bad teeth, and weed. "The cops?" He snickered. "No cops down here, bitch."

A chorus of coarse male voices echoed him. "Fuck no! Grab the bitch!"

It was all happening so fast. Eve had no time to catch her breath, to fight back. It was like someone had cut the ties to her body. She couldn't make her limbs obey. Hard hands grabbed her and threw her to the ground. The rough concrete of the sidewalk scraped her legs and hands. Her head bounced hard and she gritted her teeth not to lose consciousness. Whatever happened to her, she knew she didn't dare lose consciousness. If she did, if she lost her contact with the world, she'd just be a piece of meat to them. A sex doll. They would become even more brutal. She was in real danger here. She could die. But even if she lost her life, she was determined to go down fighting. And aware.

The man curled his hand around her necklace and tugged hard. Again, harder. It was a thin gold chain with a tiny diamond pendant, a sixteenth birthday present from her mother. He ripped it off her and she slapped him. With a growl, he punched her, hard.

In the struggle, her coat had opened. The man fisted her shirt and bra and ripped them open. Her breasts were bare. The man's eyes gleamed.

"Please," she whispered, but the breath had been

knocked out of her. Only the barest hint of sound came out. It was useless. She could plead for hours, there was no mercy to be seen in the face right above hers. He was lost to all humanity, deep in lust and violence. No pity, no mercy.

The other two men were shouting encouragement, one hopping from foot to foot, the other rubbing his crotch. He unzipped his jeans and brought out his penis, stiff and red.

"You go first and I get sloppy seconds. She looks like she'll be dry." His face was red and distorted. He looked like a demon from the furthest reaches of hell. "Keep her alive for me. No fun fucking a corpse. I like it when they fight back."

The third man knelt beside her head and held her arms down, immobilizing her. Like in some nightmare where you can't scream, can't move. Only it wasn't a nightmare, it was real.

The man on top of her pulled up her skirt, grinned when he felt she was wearing thigh highs. He ripped her panties and clutched her sex, jabbing a stiff finger in her. It hurt, burned. She could feel his erect penis against her thigh.

Eve tried to scream but, like in nightmares, only a strangled, breathless cry came out. Vomit seared the back of her throat. She swallowed heavily. She couldn't allow herself to throw up, she'd inhale it, choke. She tried to kick the man in the groin, missed. He slapped her again, hard.

"Bitch!" he hissed. "You'll pay for—"

Suddenly he was gone. As if he'd flown away. He hit the wall three feet up and fell, boneless. A dark liquid seeped out from under his head, washed away almost immediately by the driving rain.

Horrified, she rolled away. The hands grinding her

shoulders into the ground lifted and the man holding her down flew away too, as if he'd suddenly sprouted wings, cast into space.

The third man lifted a gun, but never got a chance to shoot it. It was kicked out of his hand by a tall, dark figure, who then whirled and, almost faster than Eve's eye could follow, felled him with another kick, so powerful the sound of a booted foot meeting flesh carried over the din of the rain.

Her rescuer looked up, powerful chest lifting in a deep breath. She recognized him with a surge of emotion. *Marcus Rey*. Their gazes met and held as he moved towards her.

"Look out!" Eve's voice didn't carry above the roar of the rain, but something in her face must have warned him. Another powerful whirl, a sickening thud, and the last of her assailants went down like a bull in the slaughterhouse. A fourth man she hadn't even seen.

Marcus Rey didn't look to see where the man had fallen. He had something in his hand and light strobed. Once, twice, three times, four. A second later, he was at her side, kneeling in the rain.

"Eve," he said. His voice was so deep it seemed to reverberate through her. That single word released her from her frozen terror. With a choked cry, she leaned forward into his open arms, shaking and shivering against him, burrowing hard against his broad chest. She was wheezing, as if she hadn't breathed in hours. Spots swam in front of her eyes until she had to close them and could only feel. Feel the strength of his hold, the heat of his body. One huge hand came up and held her against him and she could feel the steady beat of his heart, slow and strong. Her own heart was drumming in her chest as if it wanted to beat its way out of her body.

She barely knew him, but the violence of the attack had blown away her usual caution. At the deepest level of her being, she sensed that there was safety and shelter in this man's arms. Shaking, she tried to catch her breath. A moment ago, she feared for her life and now she felt safe.

He moved, and she didn't understand what he was doing until she felt herself enveloped by a huge overcoat. It was soft and above all warm. Even her bones seemed to shake, and she was frozen to her core. Inside that coat, with his arms around her, warmth was starting to seep in through her skin.

She burrowed against him, wanted to crawl inside his skin, knowing that here was safety and protection.

He bent his head over hers, arms holding her tight. "Shh, it's okay. You're safe now. No one's going to hurt you. You're safe, I've got you."

She barely heard the words. But her body was talking to her. The violent shudders, so hard it was as if her skin couldn't contain her, were subsiding. She could breathe. She was encased in something hard and warm and right now there was no danger to her where moments ago, she'd feared for her life. Could feel death approaching in the form of cruel violent men.

Murmuring comforting words over and over in that deep compelling voice, he slid his arms under her legs and back and stood up in a smooth, fluid motion.

Eve's head ached and the terror of the past few minutes still rushed through her. Her arms clasped his neck and she shivered, edging closer to him in her terror.

She turned her head into his neck and inhaled,

and somehow the smell of him—intensely male, yes, but worlds away from the raw feral smell of her attackers—calmed her on some deep, primitive level.

He walked swiftly, carrying her as if she weighed nothing. Her ears rang, every muscle in her body hurt and her heart was still racing with the horror of the attack. Her body was still reacting to the danger just past, adrenalin coursing through her bloodstream.

But she was safe now. Like an avenging angel come from the skies, Marcus Rey had saved her.

His even strides, the power she sensed in his arms, the strong dark planes of his face—all calmed her. She didn't know him, not really, but in some unknown way she felt she'd been waiting for him.

"You came for me," she murmured, barely aware of what she was saying.

"Yes, Eve," he said, his deep voice tender. "I came for you."

3

Marcus placed Eve gently in the passenger seat of his car and reached behind to the back seat where he kept a blanket. Spreading it over her, he tucked the edges around her shaking body, then hurried to the driver's side of the car.

Without his overcoat, he was drenched, not that he cared. What worried him was Eve. Cold and hurt and wet and in shock. She was risking pneumonia, not to mention that she might be concussed.

He turned on the engine, revved it up, turned the heat on full blast and turned Eve's seat heater up to high. Eve needed medical care as soon as possible, but she also needed to get warm. Her teeth were clacking and he could almost feel the air around her vibrate with her intense shivers.

With one last look at her, Marcus put the car in motion. He was a good driver and rarely exceeded the speed limit, but now he rocketed through the city, taking the curves dangerously fast, blessing his reflexes and the makers of the Lexus.

He knew these streets well, all the shortcuts, what to avoid. He should. He'd grown up here, in this rough part of the city, a street rat trying to survive, until he'd been able to claw his way up and out.

Paying careful attention to changing the gears and keeping the powerful car fast and steady in the high winds and driving rain, he tried not to dwell for even a second on the rage that pulsed inside him or he'd be lost. He couldn't lose control. Not now. Eve needed him.

That thought was the only thing that kept his rage from overpowering him. Just thinking about those thugs attacking her almost sent him out of control. He understood thug body language, understood it well. It was his native tongue. Those four meant to rape her, then kill her. They wouldn't have left her alive. Her last moments in this life would have been violence and violation and no one to save her.

He hadn't intended for her to see him. He'd hung out in the back of the auditorium and had followed at a distance, just to see she got home safely. In those few minutes, she'd been attacked.

His hands tightened on the steering wheel until the dark skin of his knuckles turned white. Until he took his last, dying breath, he'd never forget the sight of Eve being attacked, beaten. Clothes ripped, head slammed against the wall, about to be violently raped. Killed. The strong light that was her essence dimmed, then put out forever.

Taking another sharp corner, Marcus exited Southside onto Herbert Boulevard.

"Where... where are we going?" Eve asked.

He looked sharply at her. Her tremors had abated a little, but her face was still colorless, even her lips. She clutched the blanket tightly around her, the pale hand emerging from the soft folds of the blanket trembling.

"I'm taking you to St. Luke's. It's the closest hospital."

"No!" Eve's voice was anguished and her eyes widened in panic. "Please." She reached out with her slender hand and touched him. "Please, *please* don't take me to St. Luke's. I couldn't stand it!"

Marcus took one hand off the steering wheel and enfolded her hand in his. It was icy cold. "I have to." Why didn't she want medical care? Surely she was in shock. "You need medical attention, Eve. You're probably concussed. You were beaten. What if you're bleeding internally? A doctor's got to see you. If there's nothing wrong, you'll just check out tomorrow."

She shook her head, sliding her hand out of his. "No." Her voice was low and stark. "Please, Marcus, *please* don't take me to St. Luke's."

At any other moment, he would have been pleased to hear her say his name so naturally, as if they'd known each other for a long time, but he was too puzzled by her behavior to linger over the thought. Was it money? He could pay any amount necessary for his own medical care, so he didn't bother to carry insurance, but most people were frightened of falling sick and getting a huge bill afterwards. Even if they were insured, there were always extra costs. She worked for a streaming service. Maybe they didn't offer health insurance. Christ. He didn't want her worrying even for a second about that.

"If your insurance won't cover it, that's not an issue. Not at all. I can—"

"Insurance isn't the problem." Her voice was low, hoarse.

She bit her lips and looked away from him, outside the passenger side window. What was she looking at?

There was nothing to see but lights blurred by the cascading rain.

She was agitated, this was a thing for her, but he couldn't understand it. He waited for an explanation but there was only silence inside the vehicle. Finally, he asked, gently, "Then, what is the problem?"

Eve touched the car door window, tracing the drops falling down it on the other side. He had to let her take her time, even though he was in a fever of impatience. He wanted a doctor to look at her, make sure she was okay. He couldn't stand the thought of her being injured. It felt like a fever under his skin.

Eve took in a deep breath, as if to steady herself. "St. Luke's is where my mother died. I spent the better part of two years there, watching my mother deteriorate and die. Please don't make me go to St. Luke's," she said quietly.

"Okay." Yeah, if she'd spent a couple of years in and out of a specific hospital, watching her mother die, she wouldn't want to go there. He took a right. "Then I'll take you to The Wall -- Wallington Medical Center. It's not that much further than St. Luke's. Maybe an extra half hour's ride."

"No." Eve whispered the word. As if exhausted by her pleas, she leaned her head back against the headrest and closed her eyes. "No hospitals. I've had enough of hospitals to last me a lifetime. No doctors, no needles, no prodding, no probing. I beg of you. Please. I couldn't stand it. Just the smell of hospitals makes me sick." A tear slipped out, falling down her pale cheek. "*Please.*"

"Eve..." He didn't know how to resist her. It would have been easier if she'd ranted and railed. But that forlorn whisper and that single tear did him in. This was driving him crazy. He had to be sure she wasn't injured but she didn't want to see a doctor.

Goddammit. He was fucking holding the *fucking steering wheel.* He could drive her wherever he wanted to go and where he wanted to go was a hospital where she could be looked at. In about half an hour was the turnoff to go to The Wall. He had the map in his head. Knew exactly where to go. But... He couldn't do it. Though he did make one last try. He had to unlock his jaw, he was clenching his teeth so hard. "You might be concussed."

To him, that cinched the deal. He'd seen her take a blow to the head, then bounce off the wall of the building, before he could make it to her side. And that fuckhead about to rape her punched her in the side of her head.

If he closed his eyes, he could see it on the inside of his eyelids. Eve, being punched in the face. Eve, slammed against a wall. His hands curled hard around the steering wheel and he was surprised it didn't crack.

She refused to turn her head, continuing to stare out the window at the driving rain. Maybe she felt if she looked at him, he could convince her by the force of his will. Damn fucking straight. "If I'm concussed, there's nothing anyone can do."

"Or wounded." He was clenching his teeth so hard the words came out garbled. "You could be wounded. Adrenalin will mask the pain, but you could have a serious wound."

He knew all about adrenalin and wounds and pain. Growing up, he'd been beaten to within an inch of his life. The thought of Eve feeling that kind of pain when the adrenalin wore off made him a little crazy.

"Do you have a flashlight?"

He side-eyed her. "A flashlight?"

"Mmm. Or the flashlight app on your cell."

"Yeah. Pull up the top of the center console."

She did. He had a well-designed everything kit. She would see what was neatly arranged at the top. A Maglite, a thermos, water purification tablets, a solar charger, ten protein bars. If you lifted away the bottom, you'd also find a Glock 19, four magazines of ammo and a Tac-force stiletto knife that could cut through flesh like a knife through butter. She saw the Maglite immediately and slipped it out of its holder.

"Pull up at the next lay-by," she said quietly.

In a mile, at the next lay-by, Marcus swerved and parked. There was utter quiet in the cabin of the car. Vehicles and trucks whooshed by in the rain, plumes of water rising from the tires, but inside it was quiet and dry.

Eve turned in her seat to face him, holding out the Maglite. "I learned a lot of medicine nursing my mother and hanging out in the hospital for months at a time. It's dark in here. Shine that light in my eyes and observe carefully how quickly my eyes accommodate. Do it one eye at a time. The dilation should be the same speed and my pupils should dilate to the same size. Now shine the light in its lowest setting in my eyes."

Marcus took her chin in his hand to stabilize her and brought the flashlight up. He had to fight to keep his focus. The skin of her chin was incredibly soft, like silk. He could feel the delicate bone structure underneath. He stared into her eyes, trying not to lose himself. Though it was dark in the cabin of the vehicle, passing headlights cast enough light to turn her eyes silver. He'd never seen a color like this, close up. Her eyes were a light gray that turned silver when light flashed across it, the silver contained by a thin circle of dark gray. They seemed to glow. They were mesmerizing.

"Marcus?"

"Yeah."

"Shine the light in my eyes."

Jesus. He was a man of great focus and here he was, mooning over the color of a woman's eyes. Which was bad enough. But he was mooning over the color of her eyes when he should be checking for concussion and that was unforgiveable.

"It'll be bright," he warned.

"I know. Shine it in my left eye, then the right."

He did as he was told, rigorously not noticing how beautiful her eyes were.

"Did the pupils contract?" she asked.

"Yeah."

"Evenly? Were they the same size? Did they contract at the same speed?"

"Yeah." He said the word reluctantly. He didn't want her to be concussed, but he also didn't want to be the one to misdiagnose it.

"Signs of concussion are headache, confusion, amnesia. I'm not confused and I remember everything."

He picked up on what she hadn't said. "But you have a headache."

She was looking him straight in the eyes. "I do, but it's external, where I took a blow. Here, feel."

She took his hand and had him feel the side of her head. A quick draw of breath. "There. I'll bet you're feeling swelling."

There was. He was really sorry she had the lump from when the fuckhead slammed her into the wall, wishing he could toss him against the wall all over again. But this... his hand touching her head. It was extraordinarily... intimate. Her thick hair, smelling of roses, fell over his hand. Her scalp was warm under his fingertips. It was enthralling. Dangerous. The feel of her was making him hard, and now, by the side of a busy highway after a rape attempt, was not the time. He withdrew his hand, a heavy lock of hair sliding over the back of his hand.

She spoke, her eyes never leaving his. "The swelling will go down. Further signs of concussion are a ringing in the ears, nausea, slurred speech. I don't have a ringing in my ears. I'm not nauseous. Am I slurring my words?"

Her speech was crisp, precise. Marcus sighed. "No."

A slight smile, the first he'd seen. "I rest my case regarding concussion." She pulled up the heavy sleeve of his overcoat, pulling up her own coat sleeve and the sweater sleeve underneath. The skin was deeply abraded and there was a shallow cut. The bleeding had stopped. "I have abrasions that will need cleaning and disinfecting." She shuddered. "I feel like I need to disinfect my entire body. But that's not something that requires a hospital."

"Still. I'd feel better if a doctor saw you."

"No." She drew in a deep breath. "I'm scared and shocked and I have cuts and scrapes but nothing serious. I want to go home. God, I want to go *home*. Can't you just drive me home? The address is 1165 Crosswell Avenue. I know it's a long way, and you're a busy man. Maybe I could catch an Uber?"

Marcus was genuinely shocked, spearing her with a glance, then turning his attention back to the road. "No way in hell," he growled.

"Okay then." She turned her head against the headrest towards him and opened her eyes. They glowed silver in the dim light of the dashboard. "Please take me home." Her voice had sunk to a whisper. "Please."

She bit her bottom lip and closed her eyes again, as if she couldn't bear to watch him make his decision to hospitalize her.

He was helpless, and blew out a breath. "Okay. I'll take you home." His voice came out harsh and low. "But here's the deal. You do exactly as I say. I'll stay the night and at the first sign of something wrong, I'm bundling you up and taking you to the nearest medical center. Is that understood?"

"Yes." Her eyes opened. Her voice held a world of relief, as if his words hadn't been harsh, as if he'd given her a reprieve. When she closed her eyes again, he put in his earbuds with a tiny stem microphone. The mic picked up almost subvocal sounds. Marcus gave a verbal command to his phone. The first number on speed dial.

"Yo," a light male voice said. "Your command?"

Jorge Ramos, his indispensable right-hand man. Jorge was able to speak in an intelligible fashion thanks to the succession of operations that had repaired his cleft palate.

Marcus had first met him when Jorge tried to pick his pocket. Marcus had been a pickpocket himself and understood immediately what was happening. He grabbed the small hand, which had reached into Marcus's pocket and was pulling out his wallet.

The hand was small, the wrist tiny. He could have broken it easily. He didn't even have time to threaten the pickpocket when he fainted. From hunger. The kid was starving. He'd been born with a cleft palate and other facial deformities and his mother had abandoned him. He'd grown up in brutal foster homes and had run away from the latest one.

This he found out when he took Jorge to the infirmary. The doctor had got up in Marcus's face, saying the kid was so malnourished he'd never seen a case like that outside Africa. And an X-Ray showed he'd had almost every major bone in his body broken at one time or another.

Marcus had sighed, said he'd met the kid for the first time an hour ago, in the middle of an attempted pickpocketing. He said he'd feed the kid then release him back into the wild.

He didn't. After feeding the kid—who had an astonishing capacity for food—he realized that, though Jorge could hardly speak, he was bright. Very bright. Fifteen years and twelve operations later, Jorge was a strapping, handsome, though short young man, with a barely visible hairline scar on his upper lip and a PhD in economics which he'd earned while helping Marcus in his transition to legality. Jorge wasn't just bright, he was a genius, and he was absolutely loyal to Marcus.

"Hey. I need you to do some things for me."

"Shoot," Jorge said simply. "Anything you want." Jorge had never said no, no matter what. They'd skirted the law plenty together, as Marcus transitioned to legal businesses. But by the time Jorge came into Marcus's life, there was no longer a need to hide bodies. Marcus was sure Jorge would have done that, too, without question.

"I need some food sent to an address I'll text you. Abundant comfort food. Maybe from Mama's Kitchen. And stock my kitchen. I'll have a guest. Don't know for how long."

"Sure." Marcus had never had a guest, ever.

Marcus didn't do guests. He didn't even do people, so this was wildly unusual. But Jorge didn't say a word.

"And clear the decks for me for a while. Again, I don't know for how long. You know what to do."

"Yep."

And he did. Jorge always knew what to do.

Jorge was a genius in a lot of different fields but when it came to investing, it was like he'd invented it. Invented the very concept of money. Jorge could make money follow *him*. Over the past week, he and Marcus had plotted out their investment strategy for December. Jorge could implement it himself.

Again, if Jorge found it strange that Marcus was taking a break, he didn't say anything. Marcus never took time off, never took vacations, never not worked.

"I'm also sending photos, I want you to ID them. They almost certainly have a rap sheet. I'd ask you to ask your cop friend if they come up on facial recognition, but when they are picked up, they'll be... mangled. Wouldn't be smart."

A slight sigh at the other end. Jorge was in love with Jeff Zeldin, a young cop who'd recently been promoted to Homicide. They were just beginning a relationship, not quite a couple. And Jorge was sexually shy. He'd have found it hard to ask for a favor. Not to mention he'd have to explain why he knew about four badly wounded men. But he didn't need Zeldin. Jorge would hack into some law enforcement system and come through. He always did. "Done. I'll text you the results. Bad guys?"

"Yeah. They attacked a woman. Assault and battery and attempted rape." He could feel his jaw muscles tense, a spurt of adrenaline rush through him.

"*The* woman?" Jorge had an inkling of Marcus's obsession. Marcus said nothing.

"Man, that's bad. Is she ok?"

Was she okay? Marcus sneaked a glance to his right. Her skin was still a spectral white but that was probably the streetlamps. She wasn't huddled so tightly into herself, seemed to be more relaxed. Eyes half closed, staring out the window.

"Seems to be. It was close. Get me those names."

"Yeah, you got it."

"I'll be in touch tomorrow."

"Yeah, man. I'll be here."

"The names." Of the dead men walking. He signed off.

The rainstorm didn't abate in the hour it took him to drive to her house. He'd put in the address into the dashboard's excellent GPS, but he didn't need it. It was purely for show. He knew where she lived, and how to get there. The long drive allowed him to calm down, to climb down from the tower of terror and rage he'd felt at seeing Eve attacked. Pulling into the driveway of her building, he kept the engine running, slanting a glance at Eve.

The worst of her trembling was over but there was such a look of desolation on her face his heart clenched. "Get your keys out and ready," he said quietly.

"Keys." She blinked and stared at him blankly. Her eyes widened suddenly. "My purse!" she exclaimed. "They—"

"Here. Your cellphone's in there, too. I picked it up." He reached into the back seat and handed her the purse. It was muddy and scratched, but he was fairly sure everything was still in there. The bastards hadn't had time to rifle through it. They'd just grabbed the cell and pepper spray on top. "And your briefcase." He brought her briefcase forward, too.

"Oh." She bent her head over the purse and pulled her hand out, holding a set of keys with a silver key chain in the shape of a dolphin. The dangling dolphin shook with the trembling of her hands. She dropped it in his outstretched palm. "I seem to have a lot of things to thank you for."

Taking the keys, he kept his eyes on hers while lifting her hand to his mouth. "My pleasure."

Though wind howled outside and rain beat a tattoo on the roof and hood, utter silence reigned in the car. She stared at him, eyes wide, soft mouth slightly opened.

Slowly, he ran his thumb over her knuckles and heard her trembling sigh.

"One more thing." He slipped his hand in his pants pocket and drew out a thin gold chain with a tiny diamond pendant. The clasp was broken. Not a major piece of jewelry, but clearly of sentimental value because she started, and her eyes welled over. "Put your hand out."

She did, and he slipped the necklace into her hand. Her hand closed around it and she turned to him, blinking away the tears. "Thank you, thank you, thank you! It was a present from my mother. I would hate to have lost it."

He nodded and exited the car. Opening the passenger door, he wrapped her in the blanket and lifted her out.

In a few moments, he had her in the building and at her second-floor door. There was no alarm to set, just a lock that was pathetic. Pickable inside a minute or two. A better system was going up tomorrow.

He let her slide down until her feet touched the floor next to the overstuffed soft beige couch in the living room, and held her hand as she gingerly sat down.

"Where's the bathroom?" he asked.

"Second door to the right."

He went into the bathroom and ran hot water into the tub.

Marcus was used to taking in a situation quickly, then focusing on two, even three things at once. Keen senses had helped him rise out of Southside quickly and make a million dollars before he was twenty, though he didn't want to remember how. While depositing Eve gently on the couch, he'd observed her living quarters.

The apartment building was old, built in the 1920s. The restoration had been carefully calibrated to appeal to people whose tastes were elegant and genteel but whose budget didn't stretch to luxury.

The stairwell had been spacious, with low risers on the stairs and a graceful mahogany balustrade, but there was no elevator. The rooms were high-ceilinged and good materials had gone into their construction, but they were small. The kitchen and bathroom were standard-issue—no fancy additions such as ice makers and jacuzzis.

He knew that Eve had finished college with student loans pending and massive debts due to her mother's medical expenses. Her grandmother had died then and left Eve a house which she'd sold to help pay off her debts. The few good pieces in Eve's apartment were clearly heirlooms, the others cheap department store knock-offs which Eve brightened with throw rugs and pillows.

She had started to earn decent money from the podcasts, but there still wasn't much to spare. Especially since her leech of a father had started 'borrow-ing' money.

Marcus vowed that when their affair ended, as it had to end, he would leave Eve financially set for life.

She would never have money problems again.

EVE WATCHED WARILY as Marcus Rey walked back to where she huddled on the sofa. Nervously, she clutched the blanket more tightly about her shoulders.

She'd barely survived an encounter with four terri-fying men and here was another one, right in her living room, coming closer. He was just so huge, broad dense shoulders, massive arms that strained the sleeves of his black shirt. Long legs with powerful thighs. In her father's study, he'd had on a suit, but now that he was without an overcoat and a jacket, his unusual build was clear to see. He wasn't built like a body builder, or a gym rat, he was built like another breed of man. Taller, broader, stronger.

He was dressed entirely in black. He'd given her his huge, black overcoat and had shed his black suit jacket, so he was in a black silk shirt, black fine wool pants and highly polished black boots.

Everything about him was dark. Eyes, hair, clothes. He was fascinating—smooth dark skin, features sharp. Completely unique. She'd never seen anyone who looked remotely like him. Plus that enormous, pow-erful body moving fluidly and gracefully... it all added up to a man who was formidable. With serious fighting skills. She'd seen for herself how dangerous he was. If she lived to be a hundred, she'd never forget how quickly and effortlessly he'd overwhelmed four street punks. He was a violent man.

A violent man who'd saved her life.

Marcus stopped in front of her and hunkered down until he could look her in the eyes. Even hunkered down, he seemed enormous. His shoulders blocked the view, so all she could see was him. He lifted her chin with a long finger. His hand was hard and warm. "How are you feeling?"

Eve pulled in a breath. "Better," she said softly.

He watched her so intently it was as if he were walking inside her head. His eyes moved back and forth as he checked her eyes.

"Your pupils are the same size." He reached out, put two fingers on her wrist and waited. "Your pulse is a little fast—ninety beats a minute—but that's only to be expected after what you've been through. You don't have a temperature." He tilted her head and carefully touched the abraded skin on her cheekbones. Gently, Marcus pulled her hands and then her arms from the blanket to examine them. "Nothing needs stitches. Let me feel your head." She bent her head to his touch. It never even occurred to her not to. Probing gently, he felt through her scalp, stopping when she winced. "You've got two lumps, but the skin isn't broken. All in all, you're lucky the damage wasn't worse."

"I'm lucky you arrived when you did," she said, painfully aware of what would have happened if he hadn't. She'd have been raped and beaten up. Then probably killed. If their expressions were anything to go by, she'd have most definitely been killed. They had been ferocious, pitiless.

He shrugged. "Come on," he said softly, pulling her to her feet. Once she was up, he lifted her in his arms.

"Where are you taking me?" she asked, startled.

"You need a hot bath and something hot to eat, in that order."

He was out of luck if he wanted to feed her. The runup to the holiday season had kept her so busy she hadn't had time to do any food shopping. There was milk which expired today, half an avocado and two wizened apples in her fridge.

"I–uh. There isn't much food in the house. Sorry."

"Hmm." He didn't exactly smile, but his features lightened for a moment. "We'll see."

He carried her into the bathroom, all steamed up from her bath water. Eve realized that he'd left the door closed so the steam would cloud the air and had dumped half a bottle of bath foam into the tub. The steam and the bubbles would afford her some privacy in the tub.

"Take your clothes off and get in." The words were stark, impersonal, but a muscle was jumping in his jaw.

Eve froze. *Take your clothes off and get in.* The words were without emphasis, in that deep, deep voice of his. Calm and authoritative. But she didn't know this man, not in any real sense of the term. How could she strip with him in the room? The idea of being naked in his presence made her shiver.

Shiver in more ways than one. She had a sudden image of those large, strong hands on her bare skin and was astonished at what she suddenly felt, at the changes in her body. The hairs on the nape of her neck rose, the air in her lungs heated up so much she had to exhale fast. This shiver wasn't from cold or fear but was pure arousal.

It scared her, a reaction stronger than she'd ever had to another man, and to a *stranger*. Maybe the blow to the head had driven her temporarily insane.

She met his eyes. They were black, full of heat. The skin over his cheekbones was tight. He desired her. It was there in every line of his big body. But he wasn't making a move. In fact, he was as motionless as a statue. This was not a man out of control with lust. This was a man of massive self-control.

She was safe.

"Go ahead." He searched her eyes for a moment, then turned completely around and spoke with his back to her. "I put some shampoo on the rim of the tub. Can you wash your hair yourself?"

Eve hesitated. She was sore but she could lift her arms. "Yes."

"Then get in while the water's still warm."

She looked at that immensely broad back. She'd seen him in action. She'd felt his strength as he carried her. He could do anything he wanted with her. She looked with longing at the frothy tub, steam rising in wispy tendrils, then back to him. Shivering with nerves, she clutched her torn and tattered clothes.

He seemed to understand. "Go ahead, Eve." His voice was low and steady, as he spoke to the wall. "I'll wait until you get in. I just want to make sure the hot water doesn't make you feel faint. You could have a sharp drop in blood pressure, faint in the water." His head bowed. "Go on. I won't hurt you. I could never hurt you."

Something about his deep low voice, the bent head, the stillness of his wide shoulders reassured her. Stripping quickly, she eased into the hot water of the tub and sighed. The unease she felt at being naked with him was overridden by the relief of the hot water seeping into her sore muscles.

"Can I turn around?"

The silvery foam covered everything below her neck. "Okay."

Their gazes met. He didn't drop his eyes, didn't try to catch a glimpse of her body beneath the foam and water, but she was acutely aware of her nakedness. Her breasts ached, the warm water seemed to burn between her thighs. There was complete silence, except for the silvery sound of the bath water as she shifted.

He broke the silence. "You'll need something to put on after your bath."

She hadn't thought that far ahead. No way could she put her torn, wet clothes back on. In fact, she was going to burn them. "My bedroom is the first door on the left. There's a chest of drawers. My nightgowns are in the second drawer."

Without a word he disappeared soundlessly through the door. Eve would have liked to have breathed a sigh of relief now that he'd gone. But while he'd been in the room, she'd felt so very...safe. Scared, anxious and even—now that he was gone she could admit it to herself—aroused. All those things battling in her chest. But mostly she'd felt safe from the outside world. Safe and cared for.

Eve slipped further down in the hot, fragrant water. When was the last time she'd had someone take care of her? When was the last time she could actually just...let go? She couldn't even remember. She'd spent most of her life caring for her depressed mother, particularly in the last years when her mother had been so sick. Even her father was childish and needy. Certainly not someone she could lean on, count on. She had a couple of girlfriends, but her life had always been so busy—caring for her mother, putting herself through school, paying off medical and school debts.

There hadn't been much time for fun evenings out and there still wasn't. She rarely saw her friends.

And boyfriends? Forget it. There had never been a man in her life who put her needs before his. Who'd have fought for her, cared for her, as this dark stranger had.

No one. Until Marcus Rey.

Ack! This was ridiculous. She was being foolish, and she was *never* foolish. She was always level-headed, always doing the right thing, the reasonable thing.

What nonsense, projecting onto this man qualities she'd like him to have. It was a function of her loneliness, maybe. Loneliness came like an unexpected storm, sometimes, late at night when she couldn't stave it off. There were moments in the darkest part of the night when she felt like she was the last living human being in the world.

Well, there was an explanation for that. She'd just been attacked by four violent men. She'd *needed* saving. A one-off.

She was okay, just overtired, working way too hard. Her defenses were down. That was it. Because the fact was, she didn't need him. She didn't need *anyone*. She'd always taken care of herself just fine. Fine on her own. Marcus Rey was a stranger. Why should she imagine that Marcus Rey would be a man she could count on? Because her father knew him?

She was being foolish. Marcus Rey was a stranger. She knew nothing about him except for the fact that he was capable of dispatching a bunch of street thugs with ridiculous ease.

There were no answers.

Her head tilted back, resting on the rim of the bathtub. Her eyes drifted shut.

MARCUS ANSWERED THE DOORBELL. It was a delivery boy in uniform holding a hot heavy case.

"Here you go, sir." The kid handed Marcus the case and accepted with a smile and raised eyebrows at the Ben Franklin tip. "Wow. Thanks."

Jorge had come through. He always did. Since he'd found the broken boy fifteen years ago, Jorge had never let him down.

He'd hired tutors so Jorge could get his high school equivalency and go on to college. He'd offered Jorge a room, clean clothes, daily meals and an education in exchange for household chores, at first. Later, Jorge became his indispensable and super loyal assistant.

Like most of his instincts, this one had been rock-solid. Jorge had taken to education like a cactus soaks up rain in the desert. And like a cactus after the rains, Jorge had blossomed. The tutors could barely keep up with him.

He'd shown an unusual affinity for computers and numbers and had finished advanced degrees in math and finance while working as Marcus's right-hand man. He'd been headhunted a thousand times, had been offered jobs in academia on tenure track but hadn't even considered not working for Marcus.

Without him, Marcus didn't know if he'd have been able to manage the long, hard transition to being legit.

Jorge was the one man in the world Marcus trusted. And Jorge had shown over and over again that he was worthy of that trust.

Marcus took the heavy, warm case and called Jorge. Jorge's grim face came on.

"Food arrived. Thanks. You get a hit on those sons of bitches?"

"Yeah." Jorge nodded on the screen. "You're not going to like it."

"Probably not." There was nothing about this situation he liked. Nothing. "Shoot."

"They're part of Andrei Petrov's crew. Foot soldiers in the Bratva. Took me a while to find them because they are in the country illegally. Had to hack into Interpol."

Marcus didn't do surprise, didn't do fear. But the hairs on his forearms stood up and his heart gave a huge thump in his chest.

Andrei Petrov. Marcus had made enemies on the way up, but nothing like Petrov. They went way, way back, back to when they were starting out as violent young punks vying for territory. Petrov had been meaner, but Marcus had been smarter. Marcus had won and then had abandoned the game, slowly going legit. Petrov had been aligned with the Russian mob ruling in the city and in the Midwest and then had splintered off and founded his own crew, not without bloodshed along the way.

Their paths hadn't crossed in years, but Marcus had his sources and he knew Petrov still had a hard-on for him.

These days, Marcus was impossible to find. No one knew where he lived and Marcus had thrown a cloak of invisibility around Jorge, too. Manpower needs were taken care of by a trusted security company that was well compensated. Marcus didn't present a vulnerable flank to anyone, least of all to Petrov.

And yet, Petrov had found his weak spot. Eve. And there was only one fucking way he could have found out.

"Jorge. Check the phone records of Harrington Banner. The Fourth. As in three Harrington Banners before him. Check as of 4 p.m. Cell and landline. Find out if he called Petrov or anyone connected with him. Then stock up my house with food, like I said. The good stuff. And get the list of things I'm texting to you."

"You got it, boss. I'm—wait. Wait. *Jesus*. Harrington Banner called Petrov *directly* on his landline at 4:12 p.m. Didn't even try to hide it, or call a subordinate. Man. He's either freaking stupid or a moron. Take your pick." Jorge's sober face stared at Marcus on the monitor. "He all but called a hit on you, boss. Who is this fucker, anyway, besides some kind of trust fund asshole? *The Fourth.* Fuckhead."

Marcus shared his disdain, but over and above the disdain was rage. Pure fiery white-hot rage. Banner had called in a violent strike not against Marcus but against *his own daughter*. The man had no sense, and didn't understand what he'd done, but that was the upshot of it.

When he'd called Petrov, he must have said something to the effect that Marcus was interested in his daughter. The asshole hadn't even bothered to think it through to the next step, which was that Petrov would go through Eve to get to Marcus.

He breathed out his fury. Harrington Banner would pay for this. Marcus was going to strike a blow that wouldn't affect Eve, but Banner would pay for betraying her, his own daughter. He was going to sell Banner's debt to Claudio Martinelli, the old *capo* of the last Italian mafia clan in the state. Martinelli was not going to be like Marcus. He'd extract the money from Banner's hide, if necessary.

It was the only thing Marcus could do because he

couldn't have Eve's father whacked. Though Banner deserved it. If Marcus hadn't shown up, Eve would have been not only violently raped, but killed. Petrov didn't employ men who exercised self-control. It could have ended only in one way.

So. Banner had painted a bullseye on his daughter's back.

One of Marcus's gifts was a chess master's ability to see the next move, the one after that and the one after that. He saw clearly what had to be done. Either Eve's life would be destroyed or lost, or he had to take down Petrov.

He'd thought his violent days were behind him, he'd worked tirelessly to transition from violence, but here he was. Planning the take-down of an enemy, an enemy who threatened the one woman who meant something to him.

In the meantime, Eve had to be protected. She would not be touched by violence. The top priority.

"Jorge. I'll need someone in the Major's company to pick up a car near the Heritage Center and park it somewhere safe. I'll text the make. They won't need a key." He knew what she drove and the lowliest operative could break into the car and start it without any problems. "And then be on standby for the next few days."

"Right, boss." Jorge nodded.

"And call the Major."

Jorge's eyebrows rose. Calling in the Major was like calling in an air strike. They thought the days of calling the Major directly were behind them. But apparently not any longer. He used the Major's company and its resources, but it had been a long time since he'd had to call the Major personally.

"I want the highest level of protection around this

house possible, starting immediately. I want operators here inside half an hour. Full bore security, three perimeters. Cost no object. Protecting the woman, Eve Banner, is the objective. She must be protected no matter what. Tomorrow or the next day we will be going to my place and I want protection on the trip and once we get there. I want it invisible, but there. For at least two weeks. And have the Major assign a bodyguard to you."

In two weeks' time, Petrov would be dead. One way or another.

Jorge's face had turned to stone. He knew precisely what this meant, it meant—a return to the beginning. A return to war. To when Marcus's life was ruled by blood and iron, and each day brought new dangers. That time was gone, but now it was back. His boss was under siege by a crazy violent man.

Jorge had come into Marcus's life at the end of his war with Petrov, just as Marcus started making real money on the financial markets. Petrov thought he'd won when Marcus withdrew, leaving the marketplace wide open. He never realized Marcus had ceded the territory to him, just abandoned it.

But victory didn't slake Petrov's hatred. Petrov remembered how he'd been bested by Marcus again and again and again in the beginning and he still wanted revenge. He'd have taken his revenge before now, but Marcus was an invisible target. He had essentially disappeared from the world. And in their world, new dangers arose every day that absorbed Petrov's attention, so Marcus had dropped off his radar.

Eve's father had put Marcus back on Petrov's radar and, worse, made Eve a new target. From the days in which they'd been rivals in the street gangs, Petrov had gained in strength. He had a crew. He was known for his violence and cruelty.

In some part of what passed for a brain in Harrington Banner's head, he had heard on the grapevine that Petrov and Marcus were enemies. If he could get Petrov to eliminate Marcus, he'd have wiped his debt clean. Petrov was violent, guaranteed to hurt Marcus.

Eve's asshole of a father had aimed all that violence straight at his daughter.

Marcus was doing what he could to protect Eve. He was here, with Eve, and would stay by her side until the situation resolved itself. Nothing would hurt her— *could* hurt her—while he was alive. In a while, the perimeter of her home and to a mile out, would be protected. They would be protected on their way to his hidden home and once there, even stronger protection would be in place.

By some strange stroke of fate, Marcus was where he'd longed to be for over a year. Close to Eve. Not as close as he'd like, but still.

Yet, it was not a time for him to make a sexual move. Sex had been tainted for her by the attack. Still, he was here, with her, providing comfort, and that was enough. He knew how to wait. By a totally unexpected twist of fate, Marcus had the most desirable woman in the world, naked, in a bubble bath, not fifteen feet from where he stood.

Life is fleeting. No one knew that better than Marcus. You never knew what life held in store. Eve was here, with him. Right now, he intended to surround her with care and protection.

Marcus put the food case in the kitchen, and checked her stores. She hadn't been lying. There was almost no food in her house. He shook his head. That, too, was going to stop.

In Eve's bedroom, he pulled open the second drawer and rummaged. The nightgowns he found were made of thick, soft white cotton, most buttoned up to the neck. A nightgown more suited to a grandmother than to a desirable young woman.

He was going to buy Eve negligées in pale rose silk and in every other color of the rainbow that did justice to her delicate beauty, but for the moment he knew she'd feel better in a nightgown designed for comfort and warmth, not seduction. She'd been attacked by violent men, had nearly been raped. The last thing she'd want is to entice.

He walked back into the bathroom and stopped to look at her. Eve was dozing, her head tilted back over the rim of the bathtub, long slender neck exposed. He could see delicate collarbones, the slight swell of her breasts, one narrow knee rising out of the foam.

"Eve." He shook her shoulder gently.

Eve started violently, eyes flying open. She took in a deep breath to scream then saw it was him. He'd scared her. Instead of touching her, he should have called her from across the room.

"Oh!" Eve was breathing heavily, hands trembling. "Sorry. I—I forgot there was someone in the house." She sank further in the water.

He put a calming hand back on her shoulder. Her skin felt like satin and he gritted his teeth because what he wanted more than anything was to run his hand over the smooth skin of her shoulder, slip his hand down, cup her breast.

Soon. But not now.

"I'm sorry. I just wanted to make sure you weren't falling asleep." He still wasn't entirely certain she wasn't concussed.

She stared straight ahead, chin quivering. Remembering.

"Don't think about it. Here," he said, and opened a large bath towel. She hesitated and, with one last quicksilver glance at him, rose and stepped out of the tub and into the towel.

A silken lock of shiny red-gold-brown hair had fallen down from her topknot. It spilled over her shoulder and down to her breast. The last pale curl fell to circle her nipple, like a frame offering him her succulent breast. Both nipples were full and pink. Her nipples were erect because she'd gone from the hot bath to the relative coolness of the air in the bathroom. But he'd also seen her shudder at his look. She wasn't aware of it, but she was aroused.

Not as much as he was.

He stifled a groan as he held the large bath towel open and enveloped her in it. Her breasts brushed his chest and he had to work to keep his hands gentle.

He was painfully aroused. Fuck that bitch-goddess, fate. Six hours after meeting Eve in person, she was naked in his arms—and he couldn't act on what his entire body was clamoring for.

He was as far from making love to her as if she were on the dark side of the moon.

Every muscle was rigid with the desire to lower her to the floor and mount her immediately, slide into her warm, welcoming sheath, feeling those long, pale, slim legs hugging his waist, full breasts crushed against his chest...

He stepped back, grateful that he'd put his jacket back on. He kept his eyes on hers the whole time. "Can you make it to the kitchen?" he asked, his voice low.

At her murmured yes, he made his escape.

By the time she entered the kitchen in her granny nightgown, he'd found her dishes and cutlery and was filling a bowl with soup.

She stood framed in the doorway, shiny hair drying in tendrils about her face, eyes wide and shadowed.

His body clenched with desire to take her and wipe the sadness from her face. He wanted her to think only of the pleasure he could give her, feel only his body in hers.

Not now, he vowed to himself.

But soon. Soon.

"Sit down and eat. You'll feel better. There's a little of everything." The table was covered in food, most of it warm, all of it delicious. He had no idea what she liked so he'd had Jorge just order his favorites. Only one meat dish, since he didn't know if she was vegetarian. And there were some vegan dishes.

Minestrone, the real kind, where you could taste each vegetable. Pappardelle with Bolognese sauce, four different types of crostini, a zucchini and basil omelet, tomato salad with arugula, roasted rosemary potatoes and Mamma Gina's killer panna cotta.

She closed her eyes, drew in a deep breath, savoring the amazing smells. "Food," she breathed.

"Glorious food," Marcus answered, with a slight smile. "Come sit down. You'll feel better after you've eaten."

Eve didn't sit down. She stood for a moment, studying his face so intently he swore she would have seen into his soul if he'd had one. "You're being very... nice to me. Why is that? I hardly know you."

But he knew her. "Don't worry about that now. Eat something."

Eve continued scrutinizing his face. Finally, she

moved forward slowly and sat down. After a long moment, she picked up the spoon and dipped it into the rich-smelling minestrone. Her eyes widened. "Oh God," she moaned.

Yes, indeed. Mamma Gina had done him proud. Even though there was no Mamma Gina, there was only a genius chef, Stuart Ryan, a ginger-haired Irishman who'd studied in Bologna. The minestrone was there only to give her the strength to appreciate the pappardelle, Stuart's specialty.

When she finished the minestrone, Marcus filled a clean plate with the pappardelle and slid it over to her. "I hope you eat meat. Mamma Gina's pappardelle are famous."

She had color in her face again. "I eat meat. Not that often because it takes time to prepare, but done right..." She leaned over to smell the dish and rolled her eyes. "This smells like it's been done right."

Yep. Ryan knew what he was doing. The Bolognese sauce was simmered for a full day. "Yeah, it's done right. Here. Let me top you up."

He'd asked for two of the restaurant's finest wines and they had chosen well. The red was a Brunello di Montalcino and the white was a Piedmontese Sauvignon.

She watched him pour a generous portion of the Montalcino in her glass and then his, a little frown between her eyebrows.

Marcus sipped his wine. Excellent. He gestured at her glass. "Drink up, it'll do you good. I'm not trying to get you drunk. I'm just trying to help you relax. You've been through hell."

"I wasn't thinking that," she said. But the frown disappeared. She definitely had been thinking that. Marcus had never needed to use trickery to get a woman to share his bed. But he knew men, and knew that for a fuck with a desirable woman, a lot of men would do more or less anything, including getting a woman drunk or high.

There was total silence, broken only by Eve's fork lightly glancing off the plate and the soft sounds as they sipped the wine. Breaking bread, figuratively. Since mankind had stepped out of the caves, the best way to create ease between people was for them to share food. Marcus knew this was not the time for words, it was the time for him to provide warmth and comfort to this beautiful but traumatized woman.

He didn't need to talk, just being with her was enough. He knew her voice intimately. He'd listened to hundreds of hours of her podcasts and watched all her interviews. Now, it was just enough to be with her, feel her close to him.

It was sheer pleasure watching her. She was so amazingly classy. She ate delicately but with a growing appetite, movements graceful. Class oozed from her.

She'd once interviewed a country and western singer who'd written a book about her hardscrabble childhood in Appalachia. Eve had been sympathetic, genuinely interested. The singer/author, under Eve's gentle questioning, had proved fascinating. But the contrast between the two couldn't have been greater.

The singer had had a twang to her voice that nothing could erase and had been dressed in rhine-stones head to foot. Eve had had that Princess Grace vibe to her, dressed in a cream-colored sweater and skirt. Princess and trailer trash, clear as day. The privi-leged lady and the young girl whose truck driver stepdad drank and abused her.

And yet, nothing was further from the truth. Eve's

father had kicked her and her mother out of Waverly Mansion when Eve was ten and often forgot to pay child support. Mother and daughter had had to move into a shabby two room apartment in a bad part of town and as soon as she legally could, Eve had started working. She'd worked all through high school and had put herself through college by basically not sleeping or eating.

Not privileged at all. That class was all her. In her blood and bones.

By the time she'd finished the soup and the pasta and had two glasses of wine, color had come back into her face.

"Now the omelet," he said, cutting a wedge and putting it on another plate. "With tomato salad as a side." He spooned a few cherry tomatoes onto the plate.

Eve took in a deep breath, putting her hand over her stomach. "I don't think I can. Not another bite."

He looked at her carefully, suppressing a sigh. Women and food. He took dates to expensive restaurants all the time—always in secluded expensive private rooms—and most of them refused to eat more than a few bites. It was all show. The women looked at the food with longing, but they'd somehow trained themselves to act as if all food was poison.

Marcus hated that. People starved to death all over the world. If you were lucky enough to be in a nice place with superb food, you should enjoy it. Pretending you didn't want food because you thought you shouldn't eat was stupid and spitting in the face of good fortune.

This wasn't that. She'd eaten with pleasure, enjoying Mamma Gina's superb cooking. But she was full and didn't want any more. The omelet would be tasty for breakfast. The panna cotta too.

She was far from over the shock of the attack, but the healing, however long it would take, had begun.

"Better?" he asked quietly. She'd placed the fork on the plate, her hand resting on the table. He covered her hand with his. It trembled.

She tried to smile but it didn't work. "I tried to forget while eating that wonderful food. But—"

"But?"

"I think... I think they wanted to kill me. After raping me."

She hung her head, a few strands of drying hair falling forward over her breast. The trembling increased and she closed her eyes, clearly trying not to see again scenes of animal violence and rage and cruelty. Her breathing grew choppy. From under those ridiculously long lashes, a tear formed, fell down her cheek.

Finally.

Tears were good. Tears released stress hormones.

She was right to cry because she'd nailed it. She'd recognized the feral nature of her attackers. Marcus was sure they intended to kill her after raping her. There'd been a ferocity there that wasn't only sexual.

Marcus picked her up and carried her into the living room. He sat down on the lone armchair with her in his arms. Threading his hands through her hair, careful of her injuries, he held her tightly as she turned her face into his neck and shuddered, eyes wet.

They were the tears of a strong woman who didn't cry easily. He could hear her teeth grinding as she tried to keep her emotions in. She resisted, holding herself stiffly, shaking with the effort to keep the tears at bay.

Marcus brushed the shiny strands away from her face and leaned down. He kissed her hair so softly she couldn't feel it, then whispered into her ear. "Let go." He shifted her in his grasp to hold her more closely and she turned naturally in his arms, her head finding its spot against his shoulder. "I'll be here to catch you."

"It was... it was so horrible. Like falling through a huge hole into another world. A dark one. Those men —they were like animals, not like people. They wanted to hurt me. It was rape, but more than that, they wanted me to feel pain. To hurt. And then they wanted to kill."

Yes. She'd fallen straight through the barrier between her world and what had once been his. Where you fought like an animal for everything. Where you were predator or prey, nothing in between. And where many in that world liked inflicting pain.

He rocked her gently. "Yes. But they are not going to hurt you. They won't hurt anyone now. You're safe now. No one is going to hurt you."

Eve shook once, a deep tremor and then the tears starting coming, quickly, silently. Marcus cupped the back of her head, careful of her injuries, and gave her his warmth and his strength. They were hers for the asking.

He remembered Eve in the bathtub. The delicacy of her, the satin softness of her alabaster skin. And the bruises on her arms, the finger marks on the side of her face and neck. Marcus ground his teeth.

If he hadn't been there... but he had. He'd come just in time, stopping the worst. His hands wanted to clench into fists, clutch her tightly to himself, but he couldn't. He had strong hands and the very last thing he wanted to do was hurt her. He placed his hands, open-palmed, against her back, feeling the narrow rib cage rising and falling. He expelled his breath in a long, controlled stream to rid his body of tension.

What if he hadn't been there, hadn't been able to get to her in time? Fuck that. If there was one thing life had taught him, it was to look forward, not back. 'What if' didn't exist. Only the here and now existed.

And here and now was Eve, who needed tending.

Gradually, Eve's breathing slowed. He glanced down to see the tears drying on her cheeks, long lashes lowered, so thick they cast shadows over the delicate cheekbones. She was slumped bonelessly against him, lying in his arms. She felt delicate and soft and... right.

They sat in silence, as the storm raged outside. Lightning lit the curtains as thunder rolled loudly. Rain pattered heavily against the windows. It was a wild storm, but the cozy living room, safe from the elements, sheltered them. Eve's breathing slowed even more. Her hands had been clutching the lapels of his jacket, but her grip loosened until her palms lay against his chest.

Marcus sat and held her, long after she'd fallen into a deep sleep. One hand cradled her head, the other her back, holding her tightly.

He sat with her in his arms watching the lashing rain outside her living room window. The rain stopped and stars shone coldly down as the wind pushed the clouds away and still he held her. She was deep in the sleep of exhaustion. At the most primitive level, she knew he would keep her safe and her mind had just shut down completely to give the body rest.

Around midnight, the rain started again, drumming against the windowpanes. Later, it turned to sleet, needle sharp spicules pinging against the glass. Predictions had been for a long, cold winter, one of many in this part of the country. Winters seemed to last longer these days. Or maybe he was tired of the cold. His body craved sunshine and heat.

For a moment, he indulged himself in a little fantasy, something he never allowed himself. He'd always been able to see reality, see things for what they were. Any other attitude would have been suicide. You had to see what *was* or you wouldn't survive. He never daydreamed or wished for something that wasn't there.

But now...well, now he had the most desirable woman in the world in his arms. The past couple of hours with her, even worried about her, even if she was shocked and hurting, had been extraordinary. He couldn't remember the last time he'd felt as good.

The Major's men were outside by now, providing a protective cordon. They were the best. Petrov's men were mindless thugs in comparison to the Major's precision commandos. Nobody was going to attack him and Eve. Eve was safe in his arms, a soft warm weight he was delighted to hold.

There was time. He had nowhere to be and nothing to do that was anything as important as where he was and what he was doing. Time slowed in the darkened room. His mind was free to roam. And so Marcus indulged himself, for the first time ever. Imagining not what was, but what could be.

In that imaginary world he conjured up, he was Marcus Rey, businessman, with a perfectly respectable past. Even in his made-up world, he hadn't inherited money, he'd made it, because that was who he was. In whatever world, he'd rise to the top. In that world, he hadn't been tossed in a dumpster to die by a mother who had probably been a prostitute.

He hadn't been found and put into a brutal orphanage. He hadn't had to fight for every scrap of food and education. He'd had normal parents, had gone to school, majored in business, and had made money. In this alt-world Marcus Rey probably wasn't as rich as he was in reality, because it was hard to legally acquire the kind of wealth he'd had when he started to turn legit. But that was ok.

And in this alt-world, he'd met Eve the old-fashioned way. At a reception, perhaps. Or maybe mutual friends introduced them. Because of course he had friends in that other world. Where he'd grown up, no one had friends. They only had enemies or, occasionally, allies. Jorge was his first real friend, even though Jorge worshipped him, which wasn't a good basis for friendship.

So he'd met Eve. He'd liked her instantly because...well. Look at her. He took in the woman sleeping in his arms. Even shocked and exhausted, her beauty was evident. A heart-shaped face with fine features, straight nose, high cheekbones, full mouth.

Her eyes were closed. Light blue veins were visible in the lids. But when they were open, her eyes were spectacular. He'd never seen eyes like that—that luminous light gray with a dark band of gray surrounding it. Light caught in her eyes, and they reflected the essence of her. Her intelligence and kindness and class were immediately apparent.

A few stray hairs had fallen across her forehead. He smoothed them away, but his hand lingered in her hair. It was so soft. An amazing color made up of a thousand hues, like an artist's palette. Everything from platinum to chestnut, entirely natural. No hairdresser could possibly reproduce that color. Slowly, without disturbing her, he brought a lock to his face and breathed in the scent.

Roses. She had a rose-scented shampoo but in the alt-world...maybe she slept on rose petals. Who knew?

After being introduced, he'd make his interest known. Say he was a big fan, because it was true. Ask her out immediately. Stick by her. Never leave her side, never let another man get near her.

Because that was something that didn't make any sense to him. She seemed to be permanently single. The fuck was wrong with men? She walked through a world of men—producers of her podcast series, bankers, owners of bookshops, chefs at restaurants where she ate, doctors... What? They didn't have eyes? Didn't have hormones? It seemed to him that she should have men knocking at her door constantly, but no. Apparently not. Well, he'd knock at her door. As soon as they were introduced, he'd stay close and invite her out to dinner that evening. And the next and the one after that.

Maybe not necessarily always to the most expensive restaurants in the city. She didn't seem to be money grubbing at all, or to need expensive jewelry and status symbols. So maybe the *Chatelaine* one evening and *Mamma Gina's* the next. Then the night after, the *Pandora*, which had just won its second Michelin star. They'd sit out in the main room, in that wonderful world he was dreaming up. The alt-world.

Because in this world, the real one, Marcus took the women he fucked to the best restaurants, but never ate in the main room. He always booked one of the small private rooms all fancy restaurants had. Where politicians and movie stars and mobsters could eat without being recognized, without having to be in the crowd.

He'd love to wine and dine Eve properly. Court

her. Out in the open, proud to have her on his arm. Not hiding in the shadows, where he lived.

She stirred, eyes tracking back and forth under the delicate lids.

Another loud crack, lightning strobing the room.

Marcus rose easily from the armchair with Eve in his arms. He carried her into the bedroom, gritting his teeth as she turned instinctively towards him in her sleep. She felt so soft and light and right in his arms. The temptation to simply sink to the floor with her, pull up her night gown, spread her legs and thrust into her was almost overwhelming. He shook with a tangle of lust and something that might be... love? No. He would be taking care of his lust very soon. The love was something he couldn't allow to happen.

He placed one knee on the mattress and lowered Eve to the bed. She sighed and moved her legs restlessly. She was frowning. Was she reliving the attack in her dreams? He wanted to wipe out that frown between her eyebrows with his thumb.

Marcus sank down on the bed behind her and put his arms around her. He put his nose in her soft hair and inhaled deeply. She smelled of her rose-scented shampoo and bubble bath, of woman and the lavender sachet he'd found in her dresser drawer.

This was exactly where he'd planned to be this evening, with Eve. He'd intended to 'bump' into her after her father's introduction and invite her out to dinner. Sex would happen when it happened.

He'd happily spend evenings in her company until she welcomed him to her bed, however long that took.

She stirred, her breast fitting perfectly in his hand, her soft bottom rubbing up against him. Marcus bit his lip and resisted the urge to slide her nightgown up, lift her leg over his hip and slide into her. Instead, he held still as even more blood rushed to his dick. He couldn't remember the last time he'd been this full, this hard. He was hard as stone. Marcus tortured himself again by pressing his dick against her and clenched his teeth to stop from groaning aloud.

He wasn't a masochist, but this was the best way he knew to torment himself. Eve settled back against him.

He shouldn't be this needy. He certainly wasn't deprived. He had sex as often as he wanted. Just the other night he'd fucked an attractive woman four times and in the time it took to leave her apartment and go down in the elevator, he forgot her name. He'd felt cold and dry and empty, the fleeting pleasure of orgasm already forgotten. This was happening more and more often lately. He could fuck for hours and feel nothing.

It was in that elevator that he finally decided he needed Eve. For just a while. She'd been his far-off star, the woman who inhabited his dreams, the last thing he thought of before drifting off to sleep, the first thing he thought of in the morning. She was his obsession and he realized that he needed to live his obsession just once before dying.

It would be okay if she didn't desire him, though he knew he'd work like crazy to get her to want him. It was odd, thinking of working to get a woman to fuck him. Usually, he had no issues at all. Women didn't know who he was, but they knew he had money. For a certain kind of woman, money gave off pheromones of its own and they could smell it. He wasn't a troll, showered daily, dressed well, was reasonably attractive. And rich, on top of it all. Sex was never a problem, most especially once he became very, very rich.

But with Eve—well, he had no idea what kind of

man she liked. Nothing he knew about her led him to believe she was greedy. And maybe she liked upper class men. There was nothing upper class about him, though he had learned to imitate the manners of the rich and well born. He knew how to behave.

If she wasn't attracted... well, shit. He'd be content to spend some time with her, get to know her, at least as a friend, if not a lover. That was his thinking, before her asshole father sicced a murderous thug on her. He'd been hoping to woo her gently, take steps forward only when he saw they'd be welcome. Take it slowly. A cup of coffee with Eve, in his head, was worth fucking a dozen women.

So karma really was a bitch. Here he was in bed with Eve, who was traumatized and exhausted. In his arms. Fast asleep.

He cupped her breast gently and moved his groin against her and grew, impossibly, even harder.

It was hell.

It was heaven.

4

E ve awoke slowly, grudgingly, from the depths of a deep sleep. Dimly, she was aware of a dull, far-away noise and it took her a few moments to realize that it was the patter of rain outside the window. A steady rain, not like last night's storm. Suddenly, she stiffened as yesterday came back to her in a rush. Running late at the center. Trying to navigate her way to the car through a deluge, rain bouncing off the sidewalks, soaking her. Being slammed against the wall.

It all ran together in her memory, like a reel tape from hell. The thunderstorm, the violent brutes attacking her, the near-rape, Marcus Rey's rescue.

That, above all. Before that, the feeling of utter helplessness as the men overpowered her. It had been like fighting off wolves, immensely strong, feral. The desperation, the violence of the attack, the feeling of violation, had been sickening. And then, at the very last second, Marcus had rescued her.

In a way, he was still rescuing her.

As if he knew that waking up alone after the terrors of yesterday would frighten her all over again, she'd slept clasped in his arms, permeated by his body heat. She'd been cold all winter, it seemed. The thermometer had rarely gone above 30 degrees, day after day of unrelenting sleet, the days dark, the nights darker. Cold, cold, cold. She could never keep warm enough.

Except all through this past night. She'd been warm all night. Like sleeping next to a furnace, heat sinking through her skin to her bones, so much so that she could forget they were in the heart of a particularly brutal winter. He was behind her, big body enveloping her, wide shoulders bracketing hers. She was lying on one of his brawny arms, the other was around her waist.

She was warm and felt utterly enclosed and protected. Rising out of sleep had been in stages, slowly, as if her subconscious didn't want to face the coming day. Yet at each stage of her awakening, she'd been subconsciously aware of his protection.

However shocking and horrible yesterday's attack had been, and though it had felt like it had gone on forever, it had only lasted a few minutes before Marcus rescued her. Since then, she had been tenderly handled, even pampered.

Eve had faced many hard things in her life. Her father's abandonment, being forced to leave the only home she'd ever known. Her mother's depression and cancer and her slow and horrible death. She'd faced it all alone. There was a core of strength deep inside her. She'd recover from this ordeal, too.

But this time... this time she wasn't alone. Not being alone to face a problem was... was amazing.

She had wept her heart out on Marcus Rey's shoulder last night while he had held her tightly, one big hand covering the back of her head, his other arm around her waist in an embrace of total protection. While she'd cried, a hard knot of tension and fear, not only from the attack but from other, older sorrows, had begun to dissipate. Surrounded by a wall of strength, she'd been able to let go, as she never had before.

Eve stretched slightly... and froze at the feel of the enormous erection against her backside.

"Don't panic." The deep voice behind her was wry. Those huge arms tightened briefly, then he slid his left arm out from under her. "I've been like that all night and I haven't attacked you yet. And I won't. I'd rather rip out my own lungs than hurt you in any way. I told you that last night."

Eve turned over and blinked to find his face so close to hers. So close she could see the individual hairs of his five o'clock shadow and the exact line where his beard started. So close she could see that his irises were so dark they were almost black. So close she could feel his breath against her skin. She hadn't dared in her father's study, and last night she'd been too out of it, but now she took the time to really study him.

He'd lifted himself up to prop his head on his left hand. Though she knew he couldn't have had much sleep, he looked exactly as he had yesterday—strong and tireless and intense. His crinkly hair so short it was like a carpet over his head, precisely shaved at the forehead. His dark skin was flawless, taut over sharp cheekbones. Straight narrow nose, full lips, square jawline. Very handsome.

No, not handsome. That was a term used by movie actors and male models. He had old fashioned good looks, the kind that came from strength of character. That face could have been stamped on a Roman coin.

Suddenly, she remembered his erection, and what he'd said.

"*All night?*" she asked huskily before she could stop herself. Her eyes widened and she could feel a fiery blush bloom on her face.

"All night," he confirmed soberly. A corner of his mouth lifted and she was fascinated by the changes in his face. It was such a strong face, the features clean and sharp. That half smile made him even more wildly attractive. She was suddenly aware of her heart thumping in her chest.

"Ouch," she whispered.

"You better believe 'ouch.'" He reached out and brushed away a few strands of hair from her face. His hand was large, easily double the size of hers, lean and strong. The raised veins of an athlete coursed along them, along his muscular forearms and up the huge biceps.

Everything about this man was outsized. Leaning on his side, his shoulders were so broad he blocked her view of the window on the opposite wall. He'd taken his black silk shirt off and had a thin silk under-shirt showcasing large, hard slabs of muscle that made her stare. Beneath the silk, a mat of thick black hairs covered his chest, narrowing to a broad stripe over his flat stomach. Luckily for her heart rate, the sheet covered the rest. She'd had enough excitement for the year.

He studied her soberly and seemed pleased with what he saw. "You're looking better. Are you up for some breakfast?"

Eve wrenched her mind away from what the sheet might be covering. The memory of what she'd felt with her bottom—a long, thick column as hard as steel—made her heart thump even harder in her chest. "Yes, I—" She stopped and frowned. "Actually, um, I don't think there's anything at all for breakfast.

Not even milk. There might be some freeze-dried instant coffee. Maybe."

His eyebrows rose. "I suspect your house just grew some espresso beans and croissants. And some Greek yogurt and fresh fruit. And there's the panna cotta from last night."

She smiled. This was brand new. Since she'd been a small child alone in the house with a severely depressed woman, no one had ever prepared breakfast for her. "Is that right? Would this be from the same place that grew minestrone, pappardelle, tomato and arugula salad and Brunello di Montalcino?"

He inclined his big head. "The very same. Stay here." He bent and kissed her lightly on the lips and rolled out of bed, his movements powerful and graceful. He was out the door before she had time to react.

He'd kissed her. In her father's study she must have wondered how his kisses would taste, because her first thought was—*so that's what it's like*.

It had been the merest breath of a kiss, his firm lips just brushing hers. A touch of skin, warmth, and it was over. Yet she'd felt it down to her toes. It was like a warm hand had touched her all over, waking her body up.

The rich smell of excellent coffee wafted into the bedroom and she discovered, to her surprise, that she was hungry.

Minutes later, he walked into the bedroom carrying a tray with two steaming cups of espresso, a plate with two croissants, a tub of thick yogurt and sliced strawberries. Strawberries! And they looked like the real thing, not the pale simulacra in supermarkets. Rich, red strawberries. And...

She narrowed her eyes at the tray. "Is that milk

with *froth?* Not only do I not have milk in the house but I also don't have a frother."

He gave a mysterious smile. "The Breakfast Fairy."

Eve sat up, plumping pillows at her back. Marcus set the tray on her bedside table and sat on the edge of the bed. He unfolded a large linen napkin with a snap, placed it over her lap and handed her a cup. It was bone china with a delicate rose print.

Eve fingered the napkin. "Does my house grow linen napkins and—" she ran her hand around the rim of the cup, "Rosenthal china?"

"Limoges," he said. "Absolutely. And that same tree is going to grow some lunch in a few hours." He held up a glass of frothy milk. "Mini cappuccino?"

"God yes." She sipped the excellent coffee and milk and sighed in pleasure. "Lunch will probably be delicious, judging by this coffee, but I'll have to pass, I'm afraid. I've got a luncheon date for noon. Plus I have to go pick up my car."

"No, you don't." Marcus's deep voice was calm as he cut a bite of the croissant and lifted it into her mouth. Startled, she bit into the warm flaky pastry and nearly moaned at the buttery taste. She chewed, swallowed and frowned. "What do you mean?"

"Open up," he ordered, and held another bite before her mouth. She opened it to ask what he meant about her luncheon date and he tipped the morsel in. She chewed quickly and swallowed. "What—"

"Your car was picked up this morning and it's parked downstairs. Also, you had an appointment with Nancy Ruger at the Blue Lagoon. I called her up an hour ago and cancelled the date. She'll get back to you."

"*What?*" Eve sat up straight. "How on earth—"

"Easy. Your organizer is right on your desk. I've

cancelled all your appointments for the next three days."

Her breath caught in her throat. *The nerve!* "How dare you do that!"

His eyes glittered. "You'd better believe I dare. You need peace and quiet. The last thing you need is to go skittering around town in this weather." He gestured out the window at the gray, sullen sky and lashes of rain. "All I did was make sure you have the opportunity to get the rest you need. You need rest, Eve. One way or another I'm going to make sure that you get it." His voice was calm.

Maybe, just maybe he had a point. But she'd been making decisions for herself for a long, long time. Her voice was cold as she said, "You shouldn't have done that, made decisions for me. Or you should have at least asked me first."

"I should have. But you were sleeping." Marcus bowed his head for a moment, then lifted it. "Okay. Tell me this. What was the meeting with Nancy Ruger about?"

She opened her mouth. Closed it. "Uh...programming. For the second half of next year."

"I guess, by definition, that can be put off for a few days. What about your 11 a.m. with Rufus Seldon? Can that be postponed?"

She felt mulish, crossed her arms. "No."

"Really? He's known as a bit of a recluse. You can't do a Zoom appointment with him? I've heard he mostly videoconferences."

Her teeth ground.

"Is that correct?" Marcus tilted his head, looking her in the eyes. "Eve? Is that correct?"

Eve blew out a breath and uncrossed her arms. "Yes. I'd actually been thinking of interviewing him remotely. He apparently doesn't like going out in the cold."

He smiled. Not smugly, not like a man who'd won an argument. More like someone who was happy that something was working out. Like an adult.

She wasn't being an adult.

So, okay. Maybe he was right. Maybe she did need rest.

God knows, she hadn't been looking forward to the lunch with Nancy Ruger, an executive in the corporation that streamed her podcasts. If truth be told, she wasn't looking forward to any of the other upcoming appointments, either. She was tired and ached all over and the idea of taking it easy for a few days was immensely appealing.

How did Marcus Rey understand that?

She should be angry at him. He'd been high-handed in rearranging her life and he certainly hadn't apologized for changing her schedule. But the knowledge that he'd forced her to do something she should have had the good sense to do for herself pulled the punch of her anger.

He was watching her closely, his expression so intense the skin was pulled tightly over broad, high cheekbones. She couldn't begin to read the meaning of all that intensity, except for the fact that it was focused tightly on her.

Amazingly, even in the full light of day, the irises of his eyes were almost the same color as the pupils. She'd never seen such dark eyes before. Most dark eyes had color in them—it just didn't show up except in light. Marcus Rey's eyes looked as black as midnight.

She was staring at him. To cover her embarrassment, she took another sip of coffee.

"Is the coffee good?" he asked softly.

He had an unusual timbre to his voice. It was deep and rich, with bass undertones that set up an answering vibration in the pit of her stomach. She nodded her head jerkily.

His eyes narrowed. "Let me find out for myself."

Before she could understand his intention, he leaned forward and put his mouth over hers, slanting to open her lips. This time it was a real kiss and she shivered as his tongue met hers, sliding over it, exploring her mouth. He bit lightly at her bottom lip, licked it, then licked into her mouth. She couldn't open her eyes, she couldn't move. All she could do was open her mouth helplessly to his as his lips and tongue gave her a honeyed pleasure.

She heard a soft noise and realized, dimly, that she was moaning deep in her throat. She shook and her hands clenched in the covers. His tongue swirled deep and withdrew. His mouth lifted, settled, then lifted again. He pulled back and gazed at her. Her eyelids felt heavy; it took great effort to open them. She stared back at him, numbly.

"God yes, it's good," he whispered, and covered her mouth again.

This time she participated fully in the kiss, opening her mouth under his, raising her hands to rest them on the iron slabs of muscle on his shoulders. When his tongue met hers again, she dug her nails into his shoulders. There was no give to his skin at all. He was pure muscle.

She breathed in deeply, her nose next to his cheek and drew in a heady odor of soap and male musk. His eyes were closed and she saw that he had thick, blunt black lashes.

She couldn't see anything more because her own

eyes drifted closed. It was as if all her senses were concentrated on her mouth and she couldn't drum up enough energy to keep her eyes open.

With each beat of her heart, with each stroke of his tongue, she slid further down in the bed. Because she couldn't stay upright. Because his hard body was pressing down on hers.

He groaned and, dimly, she realized he was as affected as she was. He was hard everywhere she touched—the muscles along his shoulders, his biceps, the penis she could feel digging into her thigh.

She should draw away, but his mouth was too delicious, stroking heat into her, his taste too heady. She drifted dreamily, drugged with sexual heat as he explored her mouth.

He withdrew the barest breath away and she sighed in disappointment, but he immediately placed his lips on her jawbone and nipped lightly.

She jerked with surprise, with pleasure. Her breathing sped up as his mouth moved to her ear, where he traced the delicate whorls with his tongue.

She felt cool air on her breasts and looked down. He'd unbuttoned her nightgown and spread the wings wide.

He lifted his head and she shivered at the heat in his eyes. Arousal had turned his harsh features even starker, his normally dusky skin flushed with blood. His hand was gently stroking her breast, his thumb slowly circling her nipple.

Before the sluggish thought formed in her mind —*I should protest*—he'd bent his head to her breast and she gasped as he took the tip into his mouth.

He cupped her breast, suckling strongly, and the sensation was so intense it was like a white-hot wire drawing her towards his mouth. This wasn't a gentle suckling, like a child's, but a grown man's tugging with such strength she thought she would faint from the overwhelming sensations.

Eve looked down and found herself aroused by the contrast of his dark head on her breast.

Eve let her head fall back as he moved to her other breast. The rain had stopped, as if the world had hushed to make way for the sounds they were making —her soft pants, his harsh groans, the erotic pulling of his mouth at her breast.

She was too wrapped in a sensual haze to protest when a strong hand stroked her leg. First her calf, his hand so large it easily met around it, then the back of her knee, then slowly, slowly up the inside of her thigh. He was using his teeth and tongue on her nipple, tugging sharply and she was on fire.

At the first gentle hint of his hand, her shaking thighs fell apart.

He pressed his large, warm palm over her mound and she sighed with pleasure. Marcus lifted his head. "Look at me, Eve," he said softly. She lifted heavy lids to meet his eyes burning into hers. The air felt cool on her breasts, still wet from his mouth. He was breathing heavily, his chest expanding like a bellows. His body gave off waves of heat and hers felt as if a furnace burned just beneath her skin.

A large, blunt finger circled her flesh, stroking the folds. He couldn't help but feel her arousal, feel her hot wetness and she saw satisfaction in his lowered lids, in the flush of red over his cheekbones. His mouth was wet, lips slightly swollen from her kisses. He unfolded her as gently as a flower, petal by petal and her womb clenched.

He pushed a large finger into her heated center,

barely at the entrance, and her hips arched to take more of him.

"That's it," his low, deep voice crooned. "That's it, open for me, love."

He moved his finger deeper and circled her clitoris with his thumb. He slowly withdrew his finger and slipped a second finger in. She gave a high cry and her thighs trembled.

"God, you feel so hot and tight, love. Like a virgin. You haven't had a man in you for some time, have you?"

She couldn't breathe. She was burning up. He slid the two fingers gently in and out and then slowly separated them. She whimpered.

"Eve? How long has it been since you've had a cock here?" He thrust his fingers hard and she writhed. His fingers felt as large as a penis. Her whole body was trembling.

"Not—" she licked her lips. "Not since college."

"Good," he murmured, increasing the rhythm of his strokes. "My cock will be here soon. When you're ready. In the meantime, you're going to get used to my hands and my mouth on you. You'll come over and over again before I take you, and you'll be ready."

He circled her clitoris again, hard, and Eve exploded. She clenched helplessly around his fingers as his mouth ground into hers. Her fingers dug into his biceps as he continued stroking, harder and harder as she climaxed. She cried out, but his mouth covered her moans as she kept clenching around his fingers.

He knew just how to touch her, just how hard and how soft, to keep her on the edge, in helpless spasms of pleasure so blinding it was almost painful.

She finally subsided, exhausted, and lay back in his arms. He withdrew his fingers and touched her nipples, wetting them with her juices. He bent and licked them and she jerked. She couldn't possibly be feeling desire again, but she was.

Eve had never lost control of herself this way, hadn't known she could. It was exhilarating and frightening. She still shook with the intensity of her release. Her eyes closed and her hands fell to her sides. She could still feel the echoes of her orgasm throughout her lower body.

Marcus kissed her closed lids. "Sleep now, love," he said, and she surrendered, sliding into darkness.

5

"What is it you want from me?" Eve asked, voice harsh.

Marcus looked up from the book he'd taken from Eve's bookshelves.

He'd been pleased, but not surprised, to note that her tastes matched his. Her bookcase could have been his. He chose a book he'd read many times, noting from its well-worn look that she must have read it over and over again, too. He also suspected that, like him, she did her current reading on e-readers, and kept as paperbacks or hardbacks only the books she loved.

Eve stood in the doorway of the bedroom, eyeing him warily, too tense, too taut to move into the living room where he sat on the couch.

She held herself stiffly, arms crossed over her waist. Her face was expressionless, as if she were steeling herself against him, determined not to give in to him in any way.

He'd let her sleep the morning and the afternoon away, knowing she needed it, both for the rest it would give her body and because her mind needed downtime to process the violence yesterday.

Jorge had stopped by again leaving supplies and

Marcus could heat up a late lunch or early dinner for her at any time.

"What do I want with you?" he repeated, putting the book down, raising his eyes to hers. She stood there, the woman who haunted his dreams, rumpled, delicate, fragile. He had never been vulnerable to anyone or anything but he knew in the deepest recesses of his heart that she could bring him to his knees. "I want to fuck you," he said calmly.

She winced.

Marcus used the crudest expression to hide what he really wanted to say. His interactions with women were all, well, transactions. You give me this, I give you that. He was so used to hiding his emotions that it was second nature by now, something he realized he did naturally. With Eve, he wanted to tear it all down, rip down the walls that had always been strong and high and show himself. But now that he wanted to, he couldn't. Last night's violence had put another wall between them, his terror that something could happen to her and it would be his fault.

So he didn't say what he wanted to. *I want to love you. I want you to love me back. I want to court you, I want to win your heart, I want you to be mine forever.*

He'd come up from the dregs, from a brutal orphanage and even more brutal foster homes until he ran away at fifteen. But though he'd been born in poverty, he'd also been born strong and smart and ruthless. He'd used all the strength, power and cunning nature had invested him with to build an empire. He was rich and powerful beyond the dreams of most men. He could have anything in the world, satisfy any appetite, save one.

Eve.

He didn't truly know if he could have Eve for a lifetime.

Probably not.

He had every intention of running Petrov to ground and finishing him once and for all. But he'd made enemies in his climb to wealth and power and his enemies weren't normal businessmen. Could he keep her safe for the rest of their lives without sacrificing her freedom, her career?

Marcus didn't want to stifle her. God no. She was magnificent just the way she was—independent, having carved her own path, strong. Keeping her free and keeping her safe—could he do it?

Right now, though, he could hardly think straight with desire thrumming in his veins.

He got up and slowly walked towards her, never taking his eyes off hers. "I want to fuck you so hard and so often you'll forget what it's like not to have me inside you. I want to make you scream with pleasure, over and over again. I want to fuck you so much your body will be molded to mine, your skin smelling of me. I want you to forget where you end and I begin."

He stopped in front of her. Her eyes were huge as she scrutinized his face, as though trying to see what was behind his hard words.

He reached out to untie the knot of her bathrobe and slid it off her shoulders. It fell softly to the floor in heavy folds. Eve drew in a sharp breath, the sound loud in the silent room, but she didn't stop him.

In a moment, Marcus had the buttons of her nightgown undone to the waist. He lifted his hands to her shoulders and opened the nightgown. It slid, caught for a moment on her hips, then slithered to the floor to lie around her feet.

He wanted her more than he wanted his next breath and she wanted him back, just as much.

A lifetime of sex had taught him all about female desire. Eve didn't move, barely breathed, but she wanted him. Her cheekbones were flushed, the pupils of her eyes were so dilated only a shimmering dark silver band rimmed the black. Her nipples were deep pink and hard. He reached out with one finger to touch her.

He loved the contrast of his skin against hers. Countless times he'd read descriptions of a woman's skin, but words paled against the reality of hers. It was incredibly fine-grained, as smooth as a child's and the palest ivory in color.

As lightly as he could, he followed her slender collarbones, the swell of her breast, the smooth pink aureole a shade lighter than the nipple, down to the full, womanly underside. She was so finely made; he ground his teeth together so hard they ached at the thought of those bastards who had attacked her.

Her breasts were amazingly large for so slender a woman--heavy, firm and high with nipples that were turning a deep rose with arousal. He smoothed his hand down over her other breast and cupped it, loving the full weight of it in his hand. He bent to take her nipple into his mouth.

She liked it when he pulled hard at her. She might not even have known that she liked his mouth on her that way. He remembered her soft gasp of surprise when he'd first taken her breast in his mouth.

She didn't have much sexual experience, that was clear. His fingers had barely fit inside her and she had seemed stunned, almost frightened, at her body's response. And yet, her response to him had been strong and immediate.

There was so much he wanted to show her. He knew, from his experience with an endless number of sex partners, that when he finally took her completely, they would fit like a lock with a key. She was made for him, for his hands and his mouth and his cock.

Marcus slowly sank to one knee and gently urged her thighs apart with his hands. She had silky, ash brown hair between her thighs, soft pink flesh peeking temptingly through. He couldn't resist the temptation and leaned forward.

"Oh!" Eve swayed and Marcus clamped two hard hands on her hips as she tried to pull away.

"Not yet," he said huskily. "I need to know what you taste like here."

Like seashells, like a rose, like the dawn.

He moved his mouth gently on her, his tongue feeling the soft folds of flesh open up as he explored her sheath as thoroughly as he had explored her mouth.

He lost himself in her flesh, delighting in her soft textures, in the smell of her. For minutes, they stood there, his hands holding her up as he delved deeply into her. Suddenly, Eve gave a sharp cry and her hands clasped his head. She trembled violently and erupted in the sharp contractions of orgasm.

Marcus stood up swiftly, catching her in his arms, and carried her to the sofa.

Much as he wanted her naked in his arms, she might be cold, so he wrapped her in the soft teal blue blanket which had been draped over the sofa. Eve still trembled. She turned her face into his neck, as if she wanted to hide from him.

Marcus settled her comfortably in his embrace and lifted her chin with a finger. Her eyes were closed. The color that had tinged her face with arousal had fled and now she was pale. He waited patiently until she opened her eyes and looked at him.

"Let me tell you the way it should be in a perfect world, Eve," he told her quietly. "This is our story. It's a good one, but there are many stories like it. One night, when I'm depressed and have had too much to drink, I watch your show. You're a beautiful, intelligent woman, with a fascinating take on life. I like the way you think. I like the way you look. You love books. I love books. I get someone to introduce us and then I ask you out. Or maybe we meet at some reception for an author, or mutual friends introduce us at the theater. Doesn't matter how we meet because the attraction is instant and I ask you out immediately. On that first date, I take you to a nice restaurant and to a jazz club afterwards. I know you like jazz because you interviewed Dalton Robard, the jazz historian, and your tastes are my tastes. We have fun. There's a definite spark. Maybe you're a little lonely, too, looking for someone. God knows I'm lonely. We click on a number of levels. I take you home and kiss you goodnight. It's a good kiss, a solid kiss. Both of us would like to take it further, but it's too early yet. We both know that this is something serious, something worth taking our time over. It's not about the sex. Or, at least, not only about the sex."

Marcus bent to give her a gentle kiss on the cheek, his lips lingering over the smooth skin. When he lifted his head, he looked her straight in the eye.

"I've had a lot of sex in my life, Eve. I need it often and I've never had any trouble getting as much as I want." She was watching him carefully, intently. Her eyes, that stunning mixture of silver and dark gray, never left his. He shrugged. "Ordinarily, an hour after I've taken a woman out to dinner, I'm in bed with her.

Then we have a hot affair for a day or two. A week at the most. And on to the next one."

For a moment, Marcus rested the back of his head against the sofa and closed his eyes. Hearing himself describe his own life depressed him. He'd had all the sex he'd ever wanted but it had never been enough to fill this gnawing emptiness inside him.

For as long as he could remember, he'd refused to acknowledge his loneliness, the desire for a connection. Connections were for other people. All his life he'd thought of himself as utterly apart from the rest of humankind. He'd been born that way and, he thought, he'd die that way.

And all along, like a powerful underground river, his need for connection had flowed until it had found the right place to come up into the light.

Right now, he felt closer to Eve than he'd ever felt to any other woman. And he hadn't even been inside her yet.

It couldn't last. The connection had to be severed and his river had to dry up. But first, he was going to give himself a taste of what others thought of as their birthright—a chance at love.

Marcus opened his eyes at the feel of Eve's hand against his cheek. Her gaze was soft.

"Sounds like a lonely way to live," she said gently.

He covered her hand with his, then turned her hand around to lace his fingers through hers. He brought the back of her hand to his lips.

"Very lonely," he agreed. "Still, you can't miss what you don't know.

Only... in this perfect world, being with you, I realize exactly what it is I'm missing. What I'm missing is right in front of me. When I find you, I don't want to let you go. I take you out every night you're free. I accompany you to your conferences and lectures. I call you several times a day to find out how you are. I meet your friends and colleagues and I make it clear to everyone that I care deeply about you and that we're together. Like now, in this other world it's mid-December when I start courting you and on Christmas Day, I give you a diamond and sapphire ring and ask you to do me the honor of becoming my wife. We marry on New Year's Eve and we finally make love for the first time that night, as fireworks explode all around us."

Marcus looked at her lying in his arms. Gently, he opened the edges of a blanket a little, like opening a present to himself. Her skin shimmered like a pearl in its shell. "Man, it is so worth waiting for," he whispered.

He closed his eyes for a moment and ran his hands down her body, knowing her now by touch as well as by sight. He fondled her breasts, ran his hand over her flat belly and stroked his fingers into the notch between her legs.

"We have sex so often that you get pregnant right away. Every night we make love and every day I watch your body change as you carry our child. Late in your pregnancy, I start taking you from behind, very gently, and you feel both me and our child moving in your body." His fingers delved deeper, loving the way she grew soft and wet for him.

Eve arched, legs falling apart to ease his way. He stroked her, listening carefully to the way her breathing sped up, watching her eyes flutter.

"When our baby is born, I watch you nurse her, or him, and sometimes I feed at your breast, too, and you climax. Then you hold us both in your arms and the three of us are together, connected by love."

Eve gave a sharp cry and convulsed, contracting strongly around his fingers. His heart pounded as he turned his head to kiss her fiercely.

She clung to him and moved her bottom in his lap. He knew she could feel how aroused he was. He was as hard as a club.

Marcus lifted his lips from hers and looked down at her for a long time, letting her see his pain and regret.

"But," he said finally, harshly, "that's not the way it's going to be. This isn't a perfect world, Eve, and I haven't lived a perfect life. I've been forced to do things I regret and I've made powerful enemies, chief among them Andrei Petrov."

"But—" Eve blinked, emerging from a sensual haze. Suddenly her eyes sharpened. "But he's a member of the Bratva. A criminal, a gangster!"

"Yes, he is," Marcus agreed calmly. "And I'm not. At least I'm not a criminal any more. But, we had... dealings when I was starting out."

"He's a drug smuggler." Eve looked at him soberly. "That's what the newspapers say."

"And a trafficker and gun-runner," Marcus agreed. He wasn't about to whitewash his background but he didn't want her confusing the two of them. He was not Andrei Petrov. "I've never touched drugs, Eve and I've never trafficked. Other than that... I did what I had to do to survive. I moved on but Petrov stayed mired in the mud. I have had nothing to do with him for years. But our paths have crossed and tangled enough times to make us rivals. I bested him often and he hates my guts. He wouldn't hesitate to hurt someone who means a lot to me. That hasn't been a problem up until now."

Marcus hesitated, aware with every cell of his body

of what he was going to say. Aware he'd never said it before. Aware that he meant every word.

"No one has ever mattered to me before, Eve. I don't have any family. I have household staff but I rarely see them and they have orders to stay out of my way. I don't have personal relationships with my business associates. I'm fond of my assistant but no one knows he works for me. I have sex partners but I don't have love affairs. So I've never showed a soft underbelly to anyone. I've never been in any way vulnerable to Petrov or someone like Petrov because no one has ever meant anything to me. But now—now someone does."

She was putting it together, watching his eyes carefully. "How – how would someone put two and two together? We only met yesterday, quite casually."

Marcus stayed silent, grim and watchful.

Eve sighed. "Not so casually?"

He knew he had to be very careful here. This was exactly what he hoped wouldn't happen. "Not so casually, no. I went to visit your father to ask him to introduce us. As a—as a favor."

"You offered him money," she said flatly. "That's about the only way he'd do you a favor. He doesn't do favors. For anyone."

Bingo.

He nodded, eyes steady on hers. "Yes."

"And knowing my father…"

"He took the money. He is badly in debt." Marcus's gaze never wavered. "Yes."

"So when I walked in and he introduced us as a work colleague and friend…"

"It wasn't true. Or rather money changed hands in exchange for a specific action, so I guess it could be considered work." About as much work as Harrington Banner would ever do in this lifetime.

"And afterward?"

Marcus suppressed a sigh. "Afterward, I was hoping to engineer a meeting after one of your shows, or somewhere I knew you might be. But you mentioned being at the Heritage Center and... I guess I freaked. I just wanted to make sure you got home safely."

"I didn't. And if you hadn't been there..." Eve shuddered, a full body shake, uncontrollable. Because she, too, knew what would have happened. And then she made a leap he'd hoped she wouldn't.

"So—how would Andrei Petrov know where I'd be? And how could he know I mean anything to you?"

Marcus stayed silent. There were only the sounds of their breathing. He knew she'd already figured it out. She just didn't want to say it out loud. Finally, she sighed, looking sick.

"My father."

Marcus dipped his head. It was a terrible betrayal. He would have given anything to have her be less intelligent, to flail about. That would have been easier than her understanding the nature of her father.

Eve sat up. "*Son of a bitch.*"

Marcus dipped his head again. Yep. Son of a bitch. Marcus couldn't even imagine giving facts about his own daughter to a violent criminal. He would have sooner died. The info couldn't have been tortured out of him, either. But Banner had simply seen the possibility of making some more money. In exchange for his daughter's whereabouts and the fact that Petrov's enemy was interested in her.

Banner had put a bullseye on his daughter's back and there was no getting around that. A man betraying his daughter for money. There were no words to describe a man like that.

Eve had some color back in her face. Anger made her sit up, firm her chin. "God. I knew he was a weak man, but this... there's no excuse. I will never speak to him again."

Good. Harrington Banner didn't deserve a daughter like Eve, not in any way. He'd never been a father to her anyway.

Marcus ran his hand up and down her arm. The problems were coming hard and fast and he hated this. Hating being the one who had brought those problems to her door. But he had, and he had to protect her.

"Andrei Petrov is crazy," he said, choosing his words carefully. "Completely unbalanced. But that doesn't mean he is harmless. Far from it. He runs a gang that is at the moment flush with money and he can plan. He isn't completely sane when it comes to me, but that doesn't make him less dangerous. It makes him more dangerous."

He could read in her eyes that she wasn't connecting the dots quite yet. Eve was smart but this wasn't a question of smarts. She'd had a hard life but it had been within society's bounds. Unreliable father, sick mother... those were harsh realities but what many people faced every day. Marcus's world—ah, that was different. In his former life, the stakes were high, there were no rules, and when you lost you didn't lose just money, you lost your life. Where he came from, it was darkness and feral violence, with no rules other than to win at all costs.

So Eve wouldn't know exactly what Petrov was capable of.

But he did.

"My path hasn't crossed Petrov's path in almost fifteen years, but now that it has, and he lost—well, he's honor bound to take another run at me. I've been hard to find but now he's found me through you. I can disappear into the shadows but you can't. You're a public figure. Your livelihood depends on being seen in public and he will come at you. And whatever ideas I had about the two of us, I have to set them aside. You know that rosy scenario, the one where I court you and marry you and we live our lives together? That's for another world, not this one. In this one, if I were to marry you, I'd be signing your death sentence. You'd be a living target every day and I would go insane trying to keep you safe."

Marcus closed his eyes and the image of a broken and bleeding Eve swam against his closed eyelids. He shuddered. He opened them again and stared down at her.

"About the only way I could survive in any kind of shape would be to keep you locked up. Literally. Twenty-four/seven. Never let you out. And even then, I wouldn't feel a hundred percent secure, though where I live is a secret. But Petrov will throw money at the situation until he finds an opening. I disappeared years ago. He hasn't physically seen me in over fifteen years. But this attack on you proves that the hatred is still there. I don't doubt he would try to hurt me by hurting something I care for, and right now, Eve, that is you. He'll find some way to destroy you to get to me and just the idea makes my head explode."

She was watching him closely, as glowing and as beautiful as moonlight in his arms. He tightened his grip.

Her hand caressed his face. "And you're sure this is

Petrov's doing? It – it couldn't have been a random attack?"

Marcus looked away so she wouldn't see what was in his eyes. Pure, murderous hatred for Petrov. "God, I wish it was random, but it isn't. I took photos of your attackers' faces with my cell and sent them to a... a collaborator of mine. He's good with computers and accessed some databases—"

"Hacked, you mean," she said with a faint smile.

"Yeah, okay." He bowed his head. "Hacked. Hacked some databases. The men all have rap sheets and all are Russian. They've been here around fifteen years, emigrated here more or less when Petrov started expanding his businesses— what?" Her face had changed.

"They spoke with accents," she breathed. "Oh God. If I hadn't been so terrified, I would have noticed right away, but I didn't. How could I not have told you? I'm so sorry, Marcus, I just now remembered. The man who first hit me, almost—" she swallowed, that long slim throat bobbing, "almost raped me, he had a very heavy accent. Why didn't I tell you?"

"Because your mind tried to wipe it from your memory. You were actively trying to suppress the memory of what happened."

She was quiet a moment, breathed in, breathed out. "Yes. Exactly. But now I can look back without freaking out. And I can tell you that they definitely had accents. East European. I don't know enough to narrow it down any more than that. Could have been Russian but could also have been Ukrainian or Georgian or Moldovan."

"My informant says Russian. Most of them from St. Petersburg. All four entered on visas years ago then simply disappeared. Petrov would cover for them. Could even get them legit-looking fake IDs."

"So they work for Petrov? But you said your... relationship with Petrov was a long time ago?" she asked.

Marcus nodded.

"And you don't you think it's possible he might have... forgotten? Maybe—maybe the men who attacked me acted on their own. You were rivals a long time ago. And from what I understand, you're not in the same business at all."

Petrov had hung a rival from a meat hook and left him to die. It took two days. He was responsible for about thirty percent of the meth in the city and was moving heavily into fentanyl. Last year he'd trafficked over a thousand underage girls, placing them in brothels. Jorge said he'd heard on the grapevine that Petrov was angry because there was 'spoilage' of the merchandise. Over a hundred of the girls had killed themselves.

Not the same business at all.

"No, we're not. I'm exclusively in finance now and have left the market wide open for Petrov. But he's not the kind of man who forgets. We were kids when we started out, and were even allies, very briefly, working together to bring down the Latin Cobras. We chipped away at it, but we didn't bring the gang down. And I became sick of the constant violence, the warfare. Early on, I realized I have a good head for math and could absorb data easily. So I switched to the financial markets. Word is, Petrov wants to put his hands on my businesses. Not that he'd be able to run them. To be frank, he's not the sharpest tool in the woodshed, but he makes up in ferocity what he lacks in smarts. He's just a crazy murdering son of a bitch."

Eve listened quietly, silver eyes watching him carefully. "Surely you're smarter than he is."

Marcus's jaw worked. "Oh, yeah, I'm much smarter than he is. That's not the problem. You don't need a genius I.Q. to pull the trigger on an AK-47. You don't need to be smart to plant Semtex in a car and have it blow up at the turn of a key. All you have to be is relentless and ruthless. And you better believe that is exactly what Petrov is. The instant he realized you mean something to me; you became a target. If you were undefended, you'd be a dead woman walking." He closed his eyes briefly, then opened them again, seeing her through a fog of rage and fear. "I wouldn't be able to stand it."

Eve's face was colorless. He knew she was smart. She didn't doubt his words and he knew she could easily imagine the situation. She didn't even try to conjure up rosy scenarios, and he respected her for that.

"Is there some kind of solution to this? I can't just disappear from the face of the earth."

There was a solution. But not one he could tell her. A dead Petrov.

"No. That would be unacceptable. You need to be able to live your life. There's no question of that. I won't gamble with your safety. I want you to clear the decks for the next couple of weeks. I know you have appointments and book presentations but you need to be completely off the grid for a short while. Can you do that?"

She stared at him, unblinking. Sat up straighter. Took her time. "I could take maybe ten days off, two weeks, stretching it. And I'd take a hit because I had an appointment with a huge streaming service to talk about a new program. It's necessary to disappear?"

Marcus swallowed. He knew the streaming service, he'd seen the appointment in her agenda. The biggest there was, guaranteed to shoot her up into Oprah territory. "I wish I could say no. I wish you could continue with your life. You're on the cusp of major success and I hate it that all your hard work will take a hit. But believe me when I say you wouldn't be safe. And you could spread the word that you have a particularly nasty flu. I think I know how to guarantee your safety, but you'd have to be off the grid for a while. And the safest place I can think of is my home."

Marcus toyed with telling her the safety features, but decided against it for the moment. If you hadn't lived the life he had, it would be considered pure paranoia. Nutso territory. He wasn't nuts, but he *was* very careful.

"What will you do?"

Marcus sighed and lied. "Like I said, the only thing that gets his engine revving more than hatred is money. I will offer him a branch of my business. He won't be able to run it, but he thinks he can."

"By offer, you mean—"

"Give it to him." Marcus nodded. "Give him a branch of my business."

Her face was serious, eyebrows drawn together. "You'd do that for me?"

He tightened his grip around her waist for a moment, then relaxed his hands. If she understood what he was willing to do for her, it would scare her.

He forced himself to smile. "Definitely. And before you think that you'd be

in my debt, you wouldn't. I have... considerable holdings. This branch is something I can afford to lose. Besides, Petrov will run it into the ground inside of a year and I'll buy it back, pennies on the dollar. I'll only have lost a year's earnings from that particular business." He shrugged. "Nothing."

She was silent a moment, watching him carefully, not only listening to what he was saying, but trying to understand more from his facial expressions. Good luck with that. Marcus had learned in a very hard school never to betray emotions. He'd been in situations where any emotion, any sign of weakness, would have been punished with death. He'd learned the hard way never to tip his hand. She would get nothing from what was on his face.

"In that case, thanks." She placed her hand over his and he felt it right up to his shoulder, honeyed warmth that felt like the sun was rising in his body. "I won't deny that I was feeling scared. I don't want to live my life looking over my shoulder. Are you sure you can buy him off?"

Marcus lifted his hand and kissed the back of hers. "Absolutely. You won't ever have to worry about him."

Because Petrov would be dead. Marcus didn't intend to buy Petrov off, he intended to kill him.

6

"Are you ready?" Marcus asked quietly two days later, his hand on Eve's front door. "I want us to make it home before it starts snowing again."

Eve glanced up at Marcus standing in the darkened foyer. His face was in shadow but she didn't need light to see him. Those strong features were etched in her memory forever. Everything about him was imprinted on her consciousness, on her senses, on her skin, and would be until the day she died.

This was the first time she was leaving her house since the attack. Marcus had insisted that she needed the time to recover and he'd been right. She finally felt fully herself again.

He'd stayed by her side constantly. Three times a day, a small dark good-looking man named Jorge delivered box after box of mysterious goods, plus exquisitely prepared food and a selection of the finest wines. Marcus had insisted on feeding her himself. He'd been right there whenever she needed something. She'd almost forgotten what it was to feed herself, to bathe herself, to dress herself. For the first time in her life she'd had someone to take care of her.

She'd been utterly pampered and loved from head

to toe, over and over again. He'd used only his hands and mouth while telling her, in excruciating detail, just how he would take her completely once they were in his house. She shivered at the memory.

He glanced at her out of midnight eyes. "Cold, love?" he rumbled. "Maybe I can do something about that."

He reached down to one of the magic boxes Jorge had delivered and pulled up the sealing tape. He unfolded the flaps and pulled out something soft and blue. A flick of his hand and it billowed out—a rich silvery blue oversized cashmere coat by Valentino. He held it up. "Here, try it on."

Stunned, Eve shrugged into it, her fingers lingering over the lushly soft material. It came to mid-calf and enveloped her in soft folds of warmth.

"Marcus," she breathed. She brushed her hand down a sleeve. She'd never had anything as fine as this in her whole life. "Oh, I can't possibly—"

"Now, love." Marcus started buttoning the coat up. "I hope you're not going to say something silly like you can't accept it. Not when I sent poor Jorge all over town yesterday looking for exactly the right coat because it wasn't available online. And then I had to listen to him complaining bitterly that shopping isn't in his job description. He told me in no uncertain terms that I owe him, big time. So, after all of that, you're not going to refuse it are you?"

Eve smiled up at him and sighed. She pulled the collar of her coat around her neck, her fingers lingering over the soft material. "I guess I can't. But it's a very...extravagant gift. I don't know what to say."

"Try 'thank you,'" he suggested, taking her hands.

"Thank you."

"You're very welcome." He smiled one of his rare

smiles, lifting her hand to his mouth. "The color matches your eyes. You look so beautiful you take my breath away." He took the handle of her suitcase. "If you're ready, we can go."

The snick of the door closing echoed sharply in Eve's heart. She had a sense of a door closing on the whole first half of her life. Marcus had asked her to stay with him until he could arrange the transfer of one of his businesses to Petrov. Effectively buying her safety. It made sense to stay with him, not to mention she was looking forward to being in his domain. The man fascinated her.

She would be a changed woman the next time she walked through that door and back into her apartment.

She was a changed woman already.

Somehow, Marcus had unlocked something in her she hadn't even been aware of. It wasn't just the sex, though God knows that was shattering enough, even the foreplay he'd restricted himself to.

No, it was more than that. It was the closeness, the connection. She'd grown up with two parents who were too embroiled in their own emotional messes to pay any attention to her. And then after her father had abandoned them, she'd been so involved in coping with her mother's depression and illness that she hadn't really had time to form close friendships or even date. After her mother's death, it had taken her years of hard work to pay off the worst of the debts.

Her few affairs had been unsatisfactory and she was almost resigned to living alone and without passion.

The response Marcus had been able to effortlessly coax from her body astonished her. With him, she'd discovered a new side to her nature. An entirely new dimension to life.

It was as if she'd only gone through the motions before but now...now she was living life to the fullest. Her time with him was almost frighteningly intense.

Not to mention the fact that they connected on every level there was. He got her. He understood her in a way no one ever had. He understood what she said, what she meant. He understood what she was thinking and what she was feeling. It was like being born again.

He'd said nothing about what would happen after he'd bought her safety. Whether this was an intense short-lived affair or whether they would continue afterwards.

How would she give him up if he didn't want to continue?

Eve had grown used to Marcus, to sleeping in his strong arms, to having his mouth and hands on her, to having his tall, powerful frame as a bulwark between her and the world.

They meshed on so many levels. He'd lived rough, come up from the streets and she hadn't. She'd always had a roof over her head and enough to eat. But like him, she'd been completely on her own for a very long time. They both knew what it was like to be alone. They actually had a lot in common. Reading had saved them both. They read the same books, listened to the same music. Found the same politicians appalling. Both had the feeling the world was going to hell. They'd both done the best they could with what life had offered them.

Even after such a brief time together, Eve felt connected to this man, connected in a way she'd never felt before. What would happen if they parted ways? How would she survive?

By living minute by minute. For now, Marcus was with her, and she intended to store up memories for a lifetime.

They walked out of her apartment building and she glanced up at the sky.

It had been raining steadily for the past three days and the forecast called for heavy snowfalls over the Christmas season. The rain had stopped by the time Marcus handed her into his car, but the clouds overhead looked bruised and sullen, heavy with foreboding, like a part of Eve's heart.

Excited as she was at the thought of living with Marcus for a few precious days, of finally feeling him inside her, of being completely and fully his, she knew she was committing herself to heartbreak. Because it was entirely possible that even if he bought Andrei Petrov off, he'd still feel he represented risk for her.

"What are you thinking about?" Marcus asked as he started the engine.

Eve turned her head to study his profile. Like everything else about him, it was sharp, clean, strong. *About afterwards* she said wanted to say but didn't.

"This is the first time I've been out since–since the attack. Are we safe?"

He froze, his hands still on the steering wheel. He lifted his right hand and ran the back of his forefinger down her cheek. A small gesture, nothing compared to his hand caressing her entire body. But it was a gesture of great intimacy.

"We're safe." He bowed his head without taking his gaze from her eyes. "I have...men. A company actually. They're very good and they've been providing security since that night, around your house. We'll be accompanied to my house and while you're there, there will be a very tight cordon. You'll be safe. And you're not coming back here until I have been assured that the danger Petrov represents is over."

She mulled that over. "If your security is so tight, how come—"

"How come you were attacked?" His mouth tightened and white brackets ran down his cheeks. "That was my fault. The company provides personal security but that night I dismissed my bodyguards." He huffed out a breath. "Going to hear you speak at the Heritage Center, making sure you made it home safely...it all felt a little too personal for the Major to know about. And my miscalculation nearly cost you your life. I haven't forgiven myself yet."

She touched his hand. "The Major? You have military protection?"

"No. He's not military, at least not now. Word has it that he was—" Marcus stopped, shook his head a little, started up the engine. "Nobody really knows about the Major's past. Truth is, the Major is a mystery, but he's really good."

"We're safe, then. We won't be followed."

He didn't answer, just switched on a tablet fixed to the dashboard. At first, Eve didn't know what she was looking at, then having read a thousand thrillers informed her. She cocked her head, studying the monitor. It showed her street and the streets around her place about a mile out. The usual teardrop pinpointed their position, static, right outside her building. There was a loose circle of dots surrounding them, half static, half moving. And a looser constellation at the borders of the map.

She looked up to meet his gaze. He raised his eyebrows.

"This is a, uh," she struggled to find the words. He waited patiently. "Security perimeter."

He twirled his index finger forward. Eve frowned, looked at the screen again. Of course.

"Security perimeters."

"Bingo. You've been reading your Jack Reacher."

"I have. And the security's well done. I imagine they will sort of discreetly roam around us as we make our way to your place."

"They will indeed." Marcus started the car. The noise of the engine wasn't audible. She hadn't noticed that the night of the attack. She'd been too traumatized, too shut down to notice anything about Marcus's car that night. But now she could feel it around her like a bank vault, as if she were already in an impregnable fortress. The entire outside world felt distant, on another planet.

She touched the dashboard. Her money problems had always precluded buying a new car. She didn't like driving anyway and always had a car that was at least ten years old. This one felt like it came from ten years in the future.

"What make is this car? I don't know cars at all." She ran her finger along the dashboard, not understanding the many monitors. Even the dashboard material felt odd, something unusual.

"It's a Lexus but it has some extra features."

He pulled away from the curb and she barely felt the movement of the car. On the main screen, two red dots of the primary perimeter moved, but slowly. One dot was ahead of them. He watched her study the screen. "They know where we're going and they know the route."

She thought of every thriller she'd ever read. "You have a transponder."

"Most cars do these days. Mine is switched on, but to a frequency only the Major's company has. No one else can follow us."

She sank a little deeper into the super comfortable seat. "And I imagine you have the usual security features."

His eyes shot to the side then back at the road. It had started raining heavily. She'd be in a sweat having to drive in these conditions but he appeared unfazed. "Try me," he suggested.

"Bullet proof."

"Nothing's bullet proof but it is certainly bullet resistant. It would take an RPG to stop it. There are armored panels along the sides, the roof and the undercarriage. Anything else?"

Ok. Was this a test? "Do you have...run flat tires?"

He nodded. "Check."

"The door handles can deliver a shock in case of a carjacking."

He bit his lips to stop from smiling. "Good one. Check."

"Smoke screen dispenser."

He inclined his head. "That's good. Yes."

She was on a roll. "Night vision display."

He reached out and tapped one of the monitors. "Check."

"The Presidential limousine has a separate oxygen system in case gas canisters are thrown at it. Do you have that?"

"I thought about it, but no." He shook his head. "Adds too much to the weight which is already considerable. It would make the vehicle hard to handle at high speeds. The Presidential limousine does not speed. It can't."

"I guess we're safe."

"And going to stay that way," he agreed. "Now relax and enjoy the ride."

EVE HAD no idea where Marcus lived. He was a very rich man. She imagined he would have an upscale residence in an elegant part of town—a mansion on White Oak Drive or a luxury condo in Brixton Heights.

To her surprise, Marcus crossed the river and drove straight out to the industrial district. She tried to think of why they might be here, but drew a blank. There was nothing but dark concrete and brick buildings, huge parking lots with trucks lined up like soldiers, two-story steel fences. Most of the buildings were run down, many of the businesses were closed.

Marcus continued driving until the warehouses became scarcer, until they were driving mostly along deserted country roads, interspersed with empty lots. They never lost sight of the river to her right, a dark gray ribbon.

Across the wide, muddy river, though, was the city center. Bright lights, skyscrapers, brightly lit streets.

Ten minutes down a bumpy, deserted road flanked by bare-branched trees, Marcus pulled a remote control from his jacket and pressed a button. He slowed and she could see massive iron gates in a tall concrete wall slowly sliding back. Marcus drove through the gates and into an industrial lot.

Eve turned around. Behind them, the gates slowly closed. It was as if she were entering a different realm, leaving her old world behind.

It *was* a different realm. She could see what looked like an abandoned broken-down factory and ware-

house. Marcus pulled into what would have been the
loading bay, back when the place was a going concern.

Before her was a large structure. Only a few stories high, it was so wide she had to turn her head to
take it all in. Broken windows, cracked pavement,
weeds growing up through the cracked asphalt.
There was a desolate air of abandonment about the
place.

Eve couldn't begin to imagine what they were
doing here.

Marcus brought the car to a stop next to a steel
panel set in the wall. A halogen lamp just over the
panel was the only illumination in the entire area en-
compassed by the walls.

He got out, took her suitcase from the trunk and
came around to open her door. Taking her elbow, he
guided her to the panel in the wall. It could have been
a door, except there was no doorknob and no hinges.
It was in a better state of repair than the rest of the
building—a slab of polished blue-gray steel.

Marcus set her suitcase on the ground and pressed
his palm against a small square glass pane inserted
about five feet off the ground.

To Eve's astonishment, the pane flashed a violent
green and, a second later, the steel panel opened with
a pneumatic hiss. She swung her gaze up to Marcus
and a corner of his mouth lifted.

"Security scanner," he said, and ushered her into a
large steel cubicle.

The door hissed shut and the entire cubicle fell
quickly. She hadn't been expecting the cubicle to be
an elevator and staggered slightly. Marcus steadied
her with his hand and with another hiss, the door
opened again.

Marcus had his arm around her waist and moved

her forward by the simple expedient of stepping out himself and half-carrying her with him.

"Welcome," he said simply while she stared.

She'd never seen any place like it. Not even remotely like it.

The house had obviously been excavated out of the cliffs rising high over the south side of the river. Limestone cliffs, she remembered reading in school.

She was in an atrium at least three stories high, with a vaulted ceiling, black and white marble flooring and a striking Chinese rug. Massive enameled terracotta pots housed lemon and orange trees, ripe with fruit, stood against a wall. She could smell their clean tang from across the enormous room.

As soon as the elevator doors opened, a massive crystal chandelier lit up, banishing the gloom of the day. There would still have been enough light to see by since the entire back wall of the house was floor to ceiling windows, affording a breathtaking view of the cityscape and roiling river a hundred feet below. Eve could see the McClane Tower and the Solara Building lit up across the river.

"This is magnificent," she breathed. The atrium was several times larger than her apartment. The design, like his car, was as if transported from the future.

Marcus took her coat, tossed it on a chair. He put a hand to her back. "If you go to the right, you'll find tea waiting for you."

She didn't need to be told twice. She turned right, crossing the great hall, into what was obviously a living room. This, too, was huge, like a ballroom.

As she walked in, lamps lit up, picking up highlights. Everything she saw was luxurious and in superb taste—the artwork, the immense area rugs, Chinese vases. But everything also seemed like a one-off. Furniture she'd never seen before, stunning original artwork, lamps in unusual shapes.

The room was enormous, divided up into separate areas by the furniture, which made it feel intimate. Again, one entire wall was floor to ceiling windows. On the right wall was an enormous gas fireplace made of sandstone, easily twenty feet long, flanked by a comfortable-looking black leather sofa and matching armchairs. A fire was burning brightly and a silver tea service gleamed on a trolley.

With a sigh, Eve sat down on the sofa, held her hands out to the heat. She loved fireplaces. She hadn't had a fireplace since she had been a little girl living in her father's home.

Marcus sat next to her, placing a cut crystal decanter with an amber liquid on the coffee table. "Don't bother pouring for me," he said lazily. He poured from the decanter instead, the smell of good whiskey filling the air. "I have my own tea."

"I see you do," she smiled. Eve sipped as she watched Marcus out of the corner of her eye.

He unbuttoned his jacket and sat back with a sigh. It was the first time she'd seen him looking relaxed. Like a king who had finally come back to the palace after fighting a long war abroad.

Oddly, for a room that was both enormous and sumptuous, it was also soothing. Maybe it was the dramatic view out an entire wall, where you could watch the city at work and play, like a living painting, or maybe it was the crackling fire in a fireplace big enough to roast a herd of oxen in, or maybe just the leather sofa which was unusually comfortable, but Eve found herself slowly relaxing, too.

For the next few days—or however long it would take—she would have no cares. Nothing to do, nothing to plan. She usually had various levels of planning going on in her head. The day, the week, the month, the year, the decade. It was all gone. She was living moment to moment and the moment right now was intensely pleasurable, with this insanely attractive man watching her, ready to fulfill her desires before she knew them herself.

This house—this kingdom—was where she would spend some very intense days. She suspected she would be a changed woman at the end of her time here.

Marcus lifted her hand to his lips. "The entire house is yours while you're here," he said quietly. "Go anywhere you want, do anything you want." With the hand that held the whiskey he pointed to a console on the coffee table. "If you need anything, press the button at the top. That's for Jorge. He'll interface with the staff."

The staff. Eve looked around. Of course. A house this size would need a big staff to keep it running smoothly. "Where is everybody?"

"The next level down. Four people besides Jorge live downstairs in mini apartments. But don't worry. I relocated everyone for the duration. Everyone has strict orders to stay away. I want us to have privacy. I want to be able to make love to you anywhere, at any time. You ready to continue the tour?"

She nodded, her mouth suddenly dry at the images his words conjured up. She put her tea cup down with hands that shook and stood up on wobbly legs.

He knew the effect he had on her. That her entire body had had a flash of heat at his words and her brain had shorted. Of course, he knew. He was smart and observant. A massive arm went around her waist as he walked her around.

They went through room after room. A magnificent high-tech study with hundreds of monitors, one wall a massive screen. A truly astonishing library, with built-in bookshelves two stories high reached by wooden catwalks. A dining room like a cathedral. And always, always, the back wall floor-to-ceiling windows showcasing the city on the other side of the river. The windows had no drapes.

"Don't you wonder about privacy?" she asked. The river was wide, someone would have to take binoculars to see anything, but still.

He kissed her cheek. "No. The glass isn't transparent on the other side. It's like a one-way mirror. It's also polarized so I can blank it whenever I want to block out sunlight. And it's bulletproof."

"Resistant," she reminded him.

He bowed his head. "Yes. Bullet resistant. The closest a sniper could come is a mile across the river. And this is a turbulent stretch of river, if a sniper hired a boat, it would not be a stable platform."

She cocked her head as she studied him. This was an entirely new thought process for her. "You've thought of everything."

"Try to. If you make an error of judgment in investments, you lose some money. If you make an error of judgment in terms of security, you can pay with your life."

"But you said you were almost past that stage."

"I am. Right now, more or less the most dangerous elements of my life are changes to the euro exchange rate and the possibility of a new cryptocurrency upsetting the market. But old habits die hard. And here we are."

She was so fascinated by Marcus that she hadn't paid

much attention to where they were going. They'd been walking down a massive hallway with a magnificent geometric runner down the middle. He'd stopped outside a door. There was a clear glass panel with a keyboard.

"Put your hand against the panel."

She placed her palm against the panel. The glass was cool and smooth against her skin. A light flashed green and Marcus punched a series of numbers into the keyboard.

"Ok. I programmed the system to recognize your palm print. You are the only person besides me with unlimited access to my bedroom. To the whole house, actually."

Eve felt warmth in her chest, as if he'd just awarded her a medal. "Thanks," she whispered.

"I'll program the outside gates and entrance to recognize your palm print, too. Though we won't be going out. We're going to stay in. In this room most of the time, I hope."

He pressed his palm again and the door, which had no handle or hinges, slid into the wall and he ushered her in over the threshold.

The lights came on and Eve gasped.

Marcus looked down at her and smiled, his eyes heavy-lidded. Her thighs clenched. She knew that look. It was the look he got just before playing her body like a musical instrument. "This is the bedroom," he said softly.

It was the only room she'd seen which was carpeted. A thick, dark green mantle, like a lush lawn. Another huge fireplace, burning with some fragrant wood, was set in the left-hand wall. In the sudden hush, she could hear the crackle and pop as the resin in the wood exploded. In the far corner, so far away she thought she would need binoculars, a door opened onto rich bronze-colored tiles. A bathroom.

Louvered doors covered most of the right-hand wall. She supposed they would be the closets.

Here, too, were bookshelves everywhere, filled with what she imagined were his favorite books.

Deep burgundy leather armchairs were angled in front of the fire. There was a Louis XVI secretaire cabinet she had sighed over while reading an auction brochure, knowing she could never afford it. It had been sold for $120,000 to an anonymous bidder, she remembered reading.

At last, she turned to the bed, heart pounding. Obviously custom-made, it was easily double the size of a king, massive and... and *there*.

His voice was deep in her ear. Before she heard his voice, she could feel his heat.

"That's where we're going to spend most of our time. And most of the time we spend there, we'll be making love. I want to be inside you."

Eve's heart stuttered.

"But first," he murmured, "we have to get you settled in, calmed down. Fed. Relaxed."

She would never be relaxed again. How could she be when just the thought of what they were going to do on that oversized bed was enough to make her mouth dry and her knees tremble?

"Why don't you put on something more comfortable?" Marcus asked.

Eve swallowed and tried to get her nerves under control. "All right." She looked around. "You'll need to carry my suitcase in here, please."

He walked her toward the wall with lacquered louvered doors, a large hand at her back. "That won't be necessary." He reached around her and opened two doors wide. "I've got more or less everything you might need."

Eve blinked. The built-in closet, like everything else in the house, was huge, tall and deep. Rack after rack shimmered with the most exquisite collection of clothes she'd ever seen. She reached out a hand to touch a silver lamé evening jacket. Armani. In her size.

"The clothes are new," Marcus said quietly. "Not another woman's. I ordered them while I was at your place."

The barest glance showed that all the clothes were in styles she would have chosen herself if she'd had the money. The color palette was hers, too. Silver, all shades of blue, moss greens, pale peaches. Exquisite fabrics. She ran a hand along the clothes and felt heavy cashmeres, silks, linen. There was easily over a hundred thousand dollars' worth of clothing in that closet. Probably more.

"Is that what you were doing with your laptop?" she asked. He'd sometimes sat hunched over the keyboard while she puttered around the house. "I thought you were making megabucks on the stock market."

"I *was* making megabucks, but I was also asking the boutiques in town to scan and email me some models I thought you might like."

She looked up at him, her heart turning over in her chest at the sight of that strong, impassive face. No, not so impassive. Oddly, he looked slightly anxious, as if wondering whether she'd like what he'd done.

"They're yours," he said, placing his hands on her shoulders. "I loved shopping for you, trying to figure out what you might like. It was a real pleasure. I've never shopped for clothes for anyone else. Whatever happens…" he looked away and his jaw muscles bunched. "Whatever happens, I want you to keep the clothes."

She didn't make the mistake of protesting. She sensed this was too important to him to refuse.

Eve stepped forward, putting her arms around his strong, lean waist and leaning her head against his shoulder. Automatically, his arms went around her. "I think I'd rather keep you," she whispered.

She could feel his big body jerk and his arms tightened fiercely. He was bending down to kiss her when the black console on an English marquetry side table buzzed. With a sigh and a light kiss, Marcus released her and pressed a button.

"Yes, Jorge. I'll be right there."

Marcus turned to her, dark eyes penetrating. "I'm sorry, love. Jorge has strict instructions to contact me only if something important comes up. I have to go see what's happened. Take your time settling in. I ordered dinner to be served in the living room in front of the fire if that's okay with you. We'll meet in about an hour." His mouth tilted up in a half smile. "There's a pale pink silk knit outfit in there. I imagined you wearing it your first night here. Would you wear it for me?"

"Of course," Eve said softly. He bent to give her a swift kiss and she watched his broad back as he crossed the large room, the king on his way to check that all was well in the kingdom.

Marcus stopped at the door and turned around. "Oh, and Eve," he said, black eyes boring into hers, "don't wear any underwear."

7

"The fuck am I looking at?"

Marcus looked down at the monitors surrounding Jorge. Marcus was good with computers but Jorge was magic. He spoke to them and they answered him. All Marcus could make out was code streaming across four monitors, almost more quickly than the eye could follow. Not Jorge's eye, though.

"Here," Jorge said, his index finger touching various points of the data flow. "And here and here. Someone's trying to hack us. Whoever it is, they know what they're doing. It's subtle hacking, but it's not industrial espionage. They're not trying to uncover your investment philosophy, though that might come later. Someone's trying to find out where you actually live. They won't find anything in our files, but they're trying."

Marcus knew he'd covered his tracks very well. The ostensible owner of the abandoned warehouse topside was an offshore company wrapped in a hundred different wrappers. The records of the excellent Israeli company that had built his underground home showed construction on a site ten miles away. No paperwork connected back to him. But as Jorge said, they were trying.

"What do we do?" Jorge asked.

Marcus appreciated the 'we'. He had no doubt that Jorge took this as an assault on him personally.

He was fiercely loyal and Marcus trusted him with his life. More—with Eve's life.

"Well, find out who the hackers are, but they will be hired guns. I don't think Petrov or anyone in his entourage has the smarts to hack us. So see if you can back trace to the origins. We'll wipe out all admin data from our files. And, Jorge…"

The young man looked up. "Yeah?"

"Thanks."

Marcus had been taken off guard for the first time in his life. These were facts he should have caught himself.

It showed him what a fine line he walked. He couldn't afford distractions, ever. Much as he would like to be just an ordinary businessman, he wasn't. Not by a long shot.

The three days he'd spent wrapped up with Eve had been three days he hadn't been paying attention and he'd almost paid a hefty price. If the hackers were good, sooner or later they'd find out where he lived and attack. Petrov was on the warpath. Marcus didn't mind war with Petrov, but he couldn't afford it. Not with Eve in the line of fire.

God, how he wished his life were different. He'd been forced to do things Eve would be appalled at. But he'd done what he'd had to do to survive. He was what he was. Nothing could erase the past.

Petrov would try to come after him and anyone he loved for the rest of his life.

That was going to end. He was going after Petrov

with everything he had and he was going to put him down like a dog.

Had he held a faint glimmering of hope that he could somehow keep Eve with him forever, this turn of events had brutally plunged him back into his world. There was no place for Eve in it, certainly not with Petrov alive.

EVE WALKED into the vast living room an hour later.

She'd taken a long, luxurious bath in Marcus's amazing bathroom, so opulent it was decadent—as large as her living room and kitchen taken together. You could live in it. Easily. Happily. Put in a microwave and a futon and you were set.

The walls were made of tiny bronze tiles, the floor of sandstone. A massive bathtub, a jacuzzi. The huge glassed-in shower had a waterfall function, not to mention multiple massage jets. Again, there was the floor to ceiling window overlooking the city on the other side of the river, but between the outside window and the bathroom window was a space filled with big, healthy plants. It was like bathing in the jungle. The corners, too, were filled with plants in huge enameled vases – monsteras, fiddle leaf figs and a bird of paradise. In one corner was a magnificent lemon tree. She could smell the lemons from across the room. The overall effect wasn't 'rich guy trophy bathroom' but rather a place of rare beauty and serenity. Something told her this was a place where he unwound.

Well, she was going to unwind too. She lay in the whirlpool for almost half an hour, her head against the rim, feeling the water massaging her muscles, until the tips of her fingers started pruning.

Getting out and drying with one of the absurdly thick towels, she felt utterly relaxed and nervous. Both, at the same time. The time spent at her house had been a beginning, she understood that. As intense and as exciting as it had been, she'd barely begun to explore sex with Marcus Rey. There would be more, much more, if her heart didn't give out.

There was an ornate brass table filled with high end creams and lotions. All brands she would have happily bought if she had the money. All brand new, unopened, all clearly bought for her. With slow movements, almost in a trance, she smoothed on body lotion and face creams until her skin was smooth and fragrant and glowing.

There was a full panoply of cosmetics of various makes and colors, but she opted not to use them, and simply brushed her hair away from her face so that it fell to just below her shoulders. Looking at herself in the huge mirror over the stone sink, she tilted her head to the left and then to the right, enjoying the feeling of her hair against her naked shoulders. Usually, when she was working, she put it in a high pony tail or a bun. And she was always working.

A new woman looked at her in the mirror. She rarely looked at herself, unless it was just before the podcast, to see whether she had lettuce between her teeth or if her lipstick was on straight. She'd consulted a makeup artist early on in her career on how best to prepare for the camera, and now had applying makeup that withstood bright artificial light down pat and could apply her make up in mere minutes.

But right now, with no make-up on, she studied herself, a little amazed at what she saw. She looked... good. Not made-up TV-ready good—that was an artificial look—but normal good. With rosy cheeks, her mouth naturally curving up in a smile, skin glowing. She looked like she'd taken a long walk along the beach, then gone to the spa, then slept for twelve hours.

She looked...happy.

Eve couldn't remember the last time she'd felt happy. She was often satisfied at the end of a recording that had gone well. She enjoyed books and movies and good food. But happy?

Happy wasn't just the absence of pain and worry. Happy was something real and positive. Tangible. A *thing*. And it hadn't been part of her life for a long, long time.

She was about to embark on an affair with a man who excited her, intrigued her, challenged her. A man who made her pulse race, her skin tingle. A man who'd given her more orgasms in a couple of days than she'd had in her entire life. And they hadn't yet made love. Not fully, not completely. Just the thought of it made her smile, made her skin tingle and her heart beat faster.

Whatever happened next, however it ended, if it did end, she was grateful for this. Grateful for the surge of hopeful energy pulsing in her body. She wouldn't be surprised to see electricity crackle from her fingertips, like some superhero.

He wanted her to wear a specific outfit, some pale pink number. If it made him happy, fine. She folded back the huge closet doors and stared again.

So many beautiful clothes. Her clothes, clearly. They'd never been worn and most still had tags on them, though not prices. Good thing, too, because every item was incredibly expensive. The clothes were mostly casual, but made of cashmere, virgin wool, silk, and linen. And a rack of dresses, like magnets to her fingers. It was sheer sensual pleasure to touch them, silky and soft, beautifully made.

What Marcus wanted her to wear was obvious, a pale pink silk jersey outfit, a long skirt with a slit up the thigh with a long tunic over it. She dropped the thick bathrobe and stepped into the skirt and slid the tunic over her head. He didn't want her to wear underwear and she could feel why. The silky, slinky material was as light as air, a soft caress against her skin.

Not normally vain, she stared at herself in the mirror, turning this way and that. It flattered her, was perfectly suited to her coloring.

She felt both excited and uncertain as she made her way to the living room. Tonight they would make love fully and she could hardly contain her excitement. She breathed deeply at thought of the coming night, of finally having sex with Marcus.

Foreplay with Marcus was so exciting she sometimes thought her heart would stop. Last night she had lain naked and spread-eagled on the bed while Marcus suckled hard at her breasts, his hand moving between her thighs, for what felt like hours. She had climaxed so intensely she had actually lost consciousness for a second or two. Afterwards, she lay completely exhausted in his arms. They listened to the wild drumming of the rain outside her window. Marcus's slow stroking started turning sensual again and she had protested she had nothing left.

"Oh, yes you do," he'd whispered and brought her to another shattering climax with his hands.

He wouldn't let her touch his penis, but she'd felt it, long and thick and hard. That penis would penetrate her tonight. Finally, she'd feel him inside her.

Eve's knees weakened at the thought and she had to grab on to the back of a chair for a second. She knew his size, and his skill and her heart thudded heavily at the thought of the two of them in the heat and darkness of the night, rolling around on that massive bed.

She was wearing what he'd asked her to. The long pale pink silk skirt with the thigh-high slit whispered sensuously around her legs as she walked.

The luxury was in the delicate color and sumptuous silk knit flowing like water over her skin.

As Marcus had asked, she wasn't wearing underwear and it was like being completely naked. The smooth silky material highlighted rather than covered her body. She felt wicked and decadent, unused to feeling her breasts swaying lightly without a bra, to being able to see her own nipples, to being aware of her bare genitals as she walked.

She was aroused by the friction of the silk over her bare skin and by the thought that she was so completely accessible to his hands and his mouth.

She stopped at the enormous living room door. Through the open doorway, she could see a long table set for dinner in front of the roaring fire. A white damask tablecloth swept to the floor and a large silver candelabra with ten lit candles gave off the only light other than the fire.

She saw him across the large room and her heart rate picked up.

She would never forget the sight as long as she lived. He was in shadow, standing to the side of the massive fireplace, a large hand on the carved granite mantelpiece, the other curved around a glass of amber liquid. He was lost in thought, head bowed.

Just like that, she thought, as she committed the scene to memory. *If it ends, that's exactly how I'll remember him.*

Outlined against the fire, tall, immensely strong, graceful.

In his underground palace, he looked like a king of ancient times. A monarch of the underworld, strong and powerful but cut off from the world above. A man who commanded an invisible empire and who lived by his own rules.

As if he sensed her, Marcus's head rose suddenly and she heard his sudden intake of breath. Across the distance, his eyes met hers, shadowed and piercing, taking in every detail of her appearance.

His gaze was enough to arouse her completely. As his eyes moved down her body, she could feel her breasts swell, her nipples harden, her sheath grow moist and aching.

He started towards her, walking slowly. His boots might have made a slight noise on the stone flooring but she couldn't hear anything over the pounding of her heart. Her breathing grew shallow as he came up and stopped, so close she had to tilt her head back to meet his eyes. He took her hand and lifted it to his mouth.

"You look so beautiful in that outfit, Eve," he murmured. "Just as I knew you would." Holding her eyes, his big hand reached out and touched her breast, molding his hand around it, thumbing her nipple. "I imagined you wearing this, and me touching you, just like this. Exactly like this."

Eve's breath caught. His hand seemed to shoot fire from her breast to her womb. The feeling grew so intense it frightened her, as if he and he alone possessed the secret button to switch her on.

She had been dead, lifeless before she had met Marcus and now he seemed to have the power to catapult her into a new, frighteningly sensuous world. Her head fell back and she licked her lips as his hand caressed her other breast.

She needed to get herself back again. She straightened and pulled away, walking blindly to the huge window.

It had started to snow again, fat lazy flakes for now, drifting slowly and melting before they hit the window pane, but the weather forecast was for a heavy snowfall during the night. The night she would spend in Marcus Rey's bed.

Even more than before, she felt as if she had been sequestered by the Lord of the Underworld and taken to his subterranean fortress, spirited away from the bustling world she could see across the river.

Marcus appeared at her back, looming over her. Their eyes met in the reflection of the dark window. She looked pale, insubstantial against his dark strength. He was a head taller than she was, his shoulders almost double the width of hers. Dressed entirely in black, he was like a dark frame for her—a pale column in pink silk.

In the window, she watched him as he pulled a box from his pocket.

"Don't turn around," he whispered. Still holding her gaze in the window, he fixed an earring to her left ear, then the other to her right ear. The earrings were long pendants, a brilliant white which shone brightly in the dark pane, brighter than the floodlights of the city towers.

Eve was very much afraid they were diamonds.

"Marcus, I can't possibly—"

"Shh."

"Really, I—"

"Not a word," he murmured as he placed his hands on her shoulders, still looking at her reflection, endlessly. She felt like Persephone in Hades' kingdom, helpless in the Dark Lord's grasp.

"You're so lovely," he whispered.

Still holding her gaze, he moved his hand from her shoulder to her neck and started unbuttoning the tunic, his hand moving slowly but steadily down. With a gentle flick of his wrists, it slipped from her shoulders. He covered her breasts with his hands.

Watching him touch her and feeling his large, powerful hands caressing her breasts filled her with erotic sensations. He opened his hands and she could see her erect nipples between his fingers. Slowly, slowly, his hands ran down her rib cage, then around to her back.

She couldn't see what he was doing but she could feel and hear. The soft silk skirt loosening, then falling with a whisper to the floor. The sharp hiss of a zipper and his steely erection pressed against her back.

She was completely naked. She watched, and felt, as his hand covered her mound. He was wearing a black sweater; his powerful arm and hand bisected her white belly. Eve's breathing grew erratic as his fingers moved through the folds of her sex, stroking her, coaxing moisture from her.

Marcus bent his dark head to her neck, kissing and sucking and giving light nips that felt like electricity over her skin. Eve's legs started shaking as he inserted one long finger inside her, then two.

"I wanted to wait until after dinner," Marcus whispered, his hand moving slowly inside her. She trembled but she wasn't alone.

His hand was shaking and his breath came in low pants.

"We were going to eat, and then I was going to carry you into the bedroom, undress you slowly and love you half the night before putting my cock in you. But I can't wait," he said harshly.

Holding her apart with two fingers, he bent his knees and she could feel him sliding forward, hot, heavy, enormous, barely inside her. "Brace yourself against the window," he said hoarsely.

She stepped forward, her palms against the cool pane of glass, and cried out as he thrust into her, slowly, endlessly, until she could feel the rough hairs of his groin against her bottom. He stretched her—she could feel the tip of him pressing against her womb.

Slowly, slowly, he withdrew then thrust again, then again and again, setting up a heavy driving rhythm, one hand holding her under her breasts, while the fingers of his other hand stroked her clitoris in time with his thrusts.

He curved around her, like a massive falcon mantling its prey. She felt encased in his dark, powerful grip. The sensation was indescribable, impossibly intense. For an instant, she looked up and saw them in the reflection. She hardly recognized herself—lips puffy with arousal, eyes lost.

Her earrings and breasts swayed as he took her, moving faster and faster as he continued a driving rhythm, pounding into her.

His fingers moved sharply and Eve cried out, her orgasm so piercingly strong she thought she would die. He kept rocking inside her throughout the spasms, harder and harder until he, too, stiffened and cried out and poured himself endlessly into her.

Her heart beat in time with his and she knew she would never be the same again. Marcus was wrapped around her, still shuddering. Eve didn't know how long her legs would hold out, how long she could hold his heavy weight.

Their labored breathing sounded loud in the large, silent room.

Marcus slowly straightened, eyes closed. He pulled out of her so slowly it brought tears to her eyes at the loss. His eyes opened and met hers in the dark glass. Without taking his eyes from hers in the reflection, he pulled out a snowy white handkerchief and billowed it out. His hand went to her belly, lower. He waggled his hand, and she widened her stance. Standing like that, she could feel the cool wetness along her thighs, his juices and hers. One arm around her breasts, the other hand carefully wiped her clean. The cool stiff cloth swiped very sensitive tissues, where he'd been only a few minutes ago. She was so sensitive there, it almost—but not quite—hurt as the cloth rubbed against her.

The handkerchief fell lightly onto a glass table nearby and he bent to kiss her neck. She was so sensitized it felt like his mouth and hands had a direct line to her sex. She shivered.

"You're cold," he said softly. Stooping to pick up her clothes, he bent to kiss her neck again and then dressed her gently, as if she were a child. Pulling up the skirt and fastening it, slipping the tunic over her head. When he was done, she was perfectly presentable, but she still felt naked. As if she'd crossed into another dimension where clothes didn't exist.

Eve's muscles felt like water. She would never have been able to dress herself. She was still quivering inside.

La petite mort, the French called the moment of orgasm. The little death.

Truly, she felt as if her soul had fled her body and then had come back, transformed. Every sense was amplified—she could feel the air moving in and out of her lungs; Marcus, strong at her back; she thought she could see every snowflake now drifting in waves from the sky; she could hear the fire, the soft crackle sounding like a loud roar to her too-alive senses. The air smelled of Marcus and sex.

Gently, Marcus turned her around and walked her one step backwards, until she bumped her back against the window. His hands bracketed her face and his eyes bored into hers.

"I couldn't wait. I'm so sorry. I wanted our first time to be in bed, but I simply couldn't wait."

He bent and touched his lips to hers in the gentlest of kisses, softly, softly. Eve held on to his forearms as he kissed her endlessly, tenderly, as if it were their first kiss. As if they hadn't just had the most raw, carnal sex of her life.

Gently, slowly, the kiss went on forever. She was floating in his arms, her heart lifting. Tears pricked behind her eyelids, the sensation was so sweet. Her heart swelled as he kept the kiss light, oh so light and gentle, as if he were courting her with his mouth alone. As if he hadn't been pounding in her a few minutes before.

He lifted his mouth a moment and she remembered to breathe. "All night, Eve," he whispered against her temple. "I'm going to make love to you all night long."

Eve's hand crept up to cup his cheek. She felt so buffeted by emotions— the excitement of his lovemaking, the fierceness of his sensuality, shock at his astonishing tenderness.

"But first," he smiled, "I think I'd better feed you." Marcus took her hand and led her to the table. He seated her and lifted the silver domes covering the oversized platters. Smoked salmon. Tagliatelle with truffles and mushrooms. Blood orange and fennel salad. Ginger spare ribs. Freshly-baked five-grain bread. Wonderful smells drifted up and Eve smiled dreamily. All her senses were going to be pleased tonight. He deftly uncorked the champagne and poured.

He tapped her glass with his, the clear crystal ring of the glasses quivering in the air, and she sipped. It was icy, dry, delicious. "To us," he said softly.

"To us," she echoed. Her hand froze. *To us*. It was the first toast of that kind in her life. There'd never before been an 'us' to toast. What a sad and sobering thought.

She'd frozen just an instant, but Marcus noticed. "What's wrong?"

Eve shrugged, put on a bright smile. "Nothing. The champagne is excellent."

Marcus stopped her hand with his big one. "No. You had a thought there that bothered you. What was it?"

Oh, God. He was way too perceptive. A perceptive man was dangerous.

They sat there, looking at each other, her hand in his. Eve weighed telling the truth against telling a lie. Though something told her that Marcus was a walking lie detector. He'd probably had to be, with a rough upbringing. But the truth was embarrassing, a confession of a weakness.

He watched her steadily, warmth in those dark eyes. This was the closest she'd ever felt to another human being. What was between them was either a fiercely strong sexual attraction or something even more powerful. If she was wrong about him, he'd use her words against her. If she wasn't...maybe it would bring them closer together.

Eve wasn't a gambling woman, but she tossed the dice.

"I was thinking... I was thinking that it was the very first time someone toasted 'us.' The first time I've felt that there was an 'us' to toast." She met his eyes. "Sorry. I'm embarrassing myself. That sounds pathetic."

He brought her hand to his mouth, his breath warm over the back of her hand as he kissed it. "If it's pathetic, then I'm pathetic too. I've never toasted an 'us.' I've never been part of an 'us', either. I think this —" He waved a long finger between them, "—this is new for both of us."

She nodded slowly.

"I like it." He didn't quite smile but his features lightened from their default grim expression. "I like it a lot. I like being part of an 'us.' I never thought I would."

The only light came from the huge fireplace and the candelabra casting a warm intimate glow flickering over the table as they ate. The rest of the room was in shadow. The only noise came from the crackling, popping fire and the ting of silver against china. Outside, the snow silently swirled wildly. Eve wished suddenly, fiercely that it would just keep on snowing, for days, weeks, months. She wished they could be snowed in forever, just the two of them.

"Open up," Marcus ordered and her smiling mouth opened. They were at desert, a luscious creamy dark chocolate mousse.

Another spoonful. "Again."

Eve shook her head at the spoon heaped with chocolate. "No," she said on a sigh. Delicious as it was, she was full.

"Had enough?" His voice was a deep rumble. He put the spoon down.

"Yes, I—" Eve jumped as he pulled aside her skirt and placed a large, hard hand on the inside of her thigh. Her breath came in on a long, shaky stream as his hand moved up, then down, to caress her knee. He slowly trailed his fingers back up again and stroked the folds of her sex.

Oh God. She couldn't think when he did that. He stroked her slowly, delicately and she could feel a rush of moisture there, making her slick. His hands had worked magic on her before, when that was all she knew of making love with him. But now that she had felt his penis in her, knew how hard and thick it was, knew how it could fill her...*oh God*. She whimpered as his thumb slowly circled her clitoris.

Marcus leaned over and kissed her, his mouth slow and hot. His tongue mimicked what his hand was doing. Slowly penetrating, then retreating, leaving heat and longing in its wake.

Needing an anchor, Eve curved her hand around the strong column of his neck.

"Open for me," he whispered. She didn't know whether he meant her mouth or her legs. She opened both and was instantly rewarded. His mouth slanted over hers, biting her lips, then plunging his tongue deep into her mouth. His fingers penetrated her harder, deeper. He pulled her tightly against him as he lifted his mouth from hers. His fingers kept stroking strongly, the rhythm increasing as he watched her. Eve's mouth was open as she tried to drag more air into her lungs. She was burning up, on the knife's edge of exploding.

"Don't wear underwear while you're here. Ever." Marcus's voice was low and deep. "Wear things I can unbutton easily, pants I can open quickly, skirts I can push down. I want you open to me, day and night. I want to be able to fuck you anywhere, any time."

He circled her opening again, now completely wet with her juices. His eyes never left hers. When his thumb brushed her clitoris Eve cried out, shaking. "Marcus!"

"No! Not yet. I want you to come with me inside you." Marcus surged to his feet, sweeping her up in his arms. He strode quickly to the bedroom as she clung to him, almost too dazed to realize what was going on. The bedroom, too, was in shadows except for the fire burning in the grate. Marcus quickly stripped her and put her down on the bed. She was grateful for the cool sheets against her back. They anchored her, brought her back from the fevered place of pleasure she'd been drowning in.

Good.

She wanted to remember clearly every moment with Marcus. She'd waited twenty-eight years to feel this way and deep in her heart she knew she would never experience anything like this, ever again. She wanted to live these moments to the fullest.

Marcus looked down at her in his bed for a long moment. Eve knew that he was fixing this moment in his memory, too.

Without taking his eyes off her, he shucked off his shirt. His hands went to the buckle of his pants. Eve watched in fascination the bulge and play of muscles as he stripped, letting his clothes fall soundlessly to the thick carpet.

He was magnificent. A male animal in its prime. The power and grace evident in every line of his big body took her breath away. He was the only man alive who could turn her liquid with desire.

The fire burning at his back rimmed his body in an orange glow, like an eclipsed sun. He leaned down to grasp her ankle, as if even that short separation from her body were too much to bear. His engorged penis lay flat against the hard muscles of his abdomen, reaching almost to his navel. He was as beautiful here as he was everywhere else. He opened his hand to run his fingers along her leg, tracing her calf, trailing up her thigh, then cupping her mound.

Eve opened her arms and legs and heart. "No fore-play, Marcus," she whispered. "I don't need it. All I need is you."

With a groan, he lowered himself over her. He braced himself on his elbows, hands holding her head, and entered her with one hard thrust. She cried out in surprise and shock. He held himself still. "You okay?" he whispered.

She couldn't answer, couldn't form the words. Her body did the speaking for her as she began the sharp contractions of orgasm. He smiled down at her and started moving—slow, deep thrusts, as steady as the sea tide. His heavy movements inside her prolonged the contractions. Her thighs opened wider and she locked her ankles behind his back, her heels riding his buttocks as he moved inside her.

She was drowning in mind-numbing pleasure. Eve held him as he rode her, her arms barely reaching around the immense shoulders. The muscles along his back felt as hard as concrete slabs. A drop of sweat from his face fell on her shoulder and she opened her eyes.

Marcus's face was taut with concentration, jaw muscles bunched, eyes tightly closed. He was control-ling himself, holding himself back.

Eve turned her head and licked his ear, smiling as

he shuddered. She arched herself even more tightly against him, rubbing her nipples against his chest, rotating her hips, curling her fingernails into his back. Marcus trembled and another drop of sweat fell on the pillow.

"Let yourself go, Marcus," she whispered.

"I'm...afraid I'll hurt you," he gasped.

"The only way you can hurt me is by not loving me. Love me, Marcus, love me hard."

Her words were like a starter gun to a race horse. He bucked, then started hammering into her. She shuddered with the force of his thrusts, opening herself to him as completely as a woman can.

As she held him, as she listened to his groans, as she felt his heart pounding next to hers, she knew, with exultation and despair, that she had never been as happy as this before.

8

Out into the world, Marcus thought as he searched the depths of the glass of whiskey in his hand for solutions that weren't there. He didn't want to go, but this was for Eve's career. He was surprised at how much he wanted to simply stay home, with Eve. It was an event with interesting people, powerful people, one that, before Eve, he might even have enjoyed.

But not now. Now all he needed or wanted was her.

It was the one event on Eve's calendar that would cause her career damage if she didn't attend, because she was the guest speaker. He'd wanted to veto it, because a dead Eve couldn't be a guest speaker, but it turned out that Andrei Petrov and his top lieutenants were in Mexico, holding talks with the Michoacan Cartel about setting up a fentanyl pipeline.

Marcus had been planning with the Major. He hadn't told the Major what he wanted and the Major didn't ask, but he was no dummy. Still, Marcus's plan was to

have full intel on Petrov's movements when the time came. Petrov was due back in five days and

Marcus was ready. He hadn't lost his deadly skills. Petrov would be taken out with no collateral damage and Eve would be safe.

Jorge had assured him that Petrov was gone, and that those left in the city of his gang were the lowest foot soldiers. Jorge had even showed him footage of Andrei and twenty of his top men embarking on a private jet the Michoacan Cartel had sent for him. Jorge had followed the flight and shown Marcus footage of Andrei and his men walking down the stairs in a small airfield. Petrov stumbled getting off the plane. They all looked high or drunk.

Marcus felt safe leaving the compound.

Tonight was a commitment Eve had taken months before. She was guest speaker at the opening ceremony of the New Times Book Festival. A very big deal, particularly for someone so young.

She had offered to cancel and he'd been tempted, but she needed to move forward with her life. It wasn't fair to ask her to forego something that would further her in her career simply because he didn't want to share her with anyone.

So tonight they were going out for the first time.

He stared at the door to the bedroom, waiting for Eve to emerge. Took a sip of his whiskey. Another. Told himself that the Major's men would be tailing them, twenty of the Major's men had tickets to the event and were to provide discreet but impenetrable protection.

Petrov was away, in Mexico.

Marcus kept telling himself all this to calm himself down. Eve would be safe. She needed this evening for her career. He was being a dick wanting to just keep her home. A manipulative dick and he had to stop this, right now.

None of it helped.

He was contemplating another useless swallow when the door to the bathroom opened. Marcus looked up and his breath tangled in his throat.

She floated towards him, graceful as a princess, lovely as moonlight. She had on a long silver beaded jacket over a floor-length silver chiffon skirt, her slender legs barely visible through the layers of sheer material.

There wasn't a man alive who wouldn't try to make her his. She looked different. She walked different. Before, she'd been a beautiful but no-nonsense woman who seemed to have an invisible shield around her and a touch-me-not air. Now she was like a flame, drawing eyes to her, glowing and irresistible.

She walked up to him, unsmiling. "It's time," she said.

She had her hair up in a complicated style and had put on makeup. Already she looked different from the woman he'd shared his heart and his bed with for the past few days. The makeup emphasized that she was going back out into the world now, after having been secluded with him.

She was going back out into the world where men would look at her and desire her.

Eve's eyes widened as Marcus put his arms around her.

"Marcus?"

He couldn't touch her hair, kiss her mouth, as he wanted to. He could only touch her where it wouldn't show. He stroked the soft skin of her neck and felt the life pulsing through a vein. How many times had he touched her, caressed her, stroking, feeling her skin warm under his touch?

"Yes," she murmured, knowing from his touch

what he wanted. She exhaled softly, her head falling slightly to one side, a rose too heavy for its stem.

He reached out to unbutton her jacket and her eyes closed. "Eve." His voice was the merest whisper as he slid the jacket off her shoulders. It fell soundlessly to the carpet and her lace bra followed.

He cupped her breasts. He loved the heavy feel of them and had spent hours fondling them, suckling them. Her eyes closed as his thumbs rubbed over her nipples.

"Christ, you're lovely." His voice came out low and rough.

When they came back tonight, he intended to get in her and stay in her all night but now, right now, his hunger was sharp-edged, as if he'd never had her and would die if he couldn't enter her *now*.

He couldn't get the image of another man's hands touching her, another man's cock inside her, out of his head. It drove him crazy and his hands turned rough as he opened her skirt and pushed it down.

She had on sheer silk stockings held up with lace garters and panties. With a low, maddened growl, he ripped her panties off and pulled her to him. He turned with her held in one arm. With the other he swept the table clear. A vase and books thudded to the carpet but he was beyond caring as he lay her down on the smooth cherrywood surface.

He stopped a moment, checked by the sight of her long pale figure laid out like a sacrifice, naked except for the garter belt, the stockings and strappy sandals. He was hard as a rock, his penis straining to be inside her. "I need you, Eve," he muttered, opening her legs by stepping between them. "I need you so much."

Her eyes opened and their gazes locked. "I'm yours, Marcus," she whispered. "I always will be."

His own eyes closed in pain. His hands shook as they traveled up her long legs. His thumbs opened her and he dropped to his knees.

She was as beautiful here as she was everywhere else, smooth folds of skin surrounded by fine ash brown hairs. The pale pink lips he'd entered countless times slowly deepened in color as he stroked her gently. He watched as his fingers coaxed the cream of arousal from her. Her back arched and she moaned as he slid first one finger then a second finger into her, touching her as he knew she loved to be touched.

He brought his mouth to her and heard her sharp intake of breath. He kissed her deeply, exactly as if he were kissing her mouth. His tongue circled her clitoris then slid lower to plunge back into her vagina. His thumbs opened her wider as his tongue imitated his dick. Eve's thighs shook and she suddenly cried out and pulsed against his mouth. He could feel, taste her climax. Rising swiftly, he opened his pants and thrust into her hard, gritting his teeth to keep still as she continued climaxing.

She'd thrown her arms up over her head and lay stretched out before him, pale and slender, impaled on his dick. Her breasts shook with the force of her wildly beating heart. The pulsing of her vagina matched her pulse beats and he could feel himself become impossibly harder inside her.

As the contractions faded away, Eve opened her eyes. "God, Marcus," she whispered, sounding dazed.

"Rise up," he said harshly and waited until she levered herself up on her elbows. "Look at us." He used his thumbs to open her more fully to his gaze and hers. "Look."

Flexing his buttocks, he pushed with the force of his hips until he felt the tip of her womb. He clenched his jaw and pushed further. The hairs at the root of his sex meshed with hers, jet black and light brown. He ground against her, opening her up even more to his possession. "Mine," he gritted, his voice guttural. "All mine."

"Yours," Eve breathed.

They stared at each other, joined in every way a man and a woman could be joined, sex to sex, heart to heart, gaze to gaze.

Marcus was the first to look away. He closed his eyes and leaned back. His hands gripped her hips hard enough to bruise and he began thrusting with all the strength of his body, hard and fast, in a hammering rhythm which he knew would have hurt her if she hadn't already climaxed. For all the force of his thrusts, he could feel her sheath soft and wet and welcoming.

His passion was too violent to last. A hot wire flashed down his spine, his back prickled, it was as if a freight train barreled into him and he erupted in her, jetting in wild spurts so intense he shuddered under the impact. His orgasm seemed to last for hours as he shook and groaned and spilled into her.

His knees were trembling as he pulled slowly out of her. Amazingly, he was still semi-erect even after that shattering orgasm. He could never get enough of Eve.

Capable of gentleness at last, his fingers closed over hers and he pulled her slowly up. Her fingers clutched his, silver eyes wide in a pale face. She'd been as affected as he had by the intense sex. A pulse beat wildly in her throat. He lowered his lips to lick along the vein, teeth closing on the nerve in her neck. Eve arched, moaning.

Marcus slid his other hand around her back and down to her buttocks, helping her off the table.

"We have to go out into the world."

"I know." She shuddered.

His voice was strained to make its way past the constriction in his throat. "Men will look at you tonight, but you're not going to be aware of them. You're only going to be aware of *me*." He bent to pick up the beaded jacket, ignoring her bra which had fallen nearby. He slipped the jacket up her arms and paused. Arching her over his arm, he suckled slowly at one breast, then the other. When he finally lifted his head, her nipples were wet and distended, flushed a deep pink. He pulled the jacket up over her shoulders and buttoned it, his knuckles brushing against the soft skin of her breasts.

"They'll be talking to you and you won't hear a word because you'll be feeling your nipples against the material all night. All you'll be able to think about is my mouth on you, sucking hard."

She drew in a sharp breath.

He kicked away her torn panties and held her skirt open. Shakily, she stepped into it, one hand on his shoulder to balance herself.

Marcus slid his hand under the skirt and felt his semen on her thighs. "And all evening," he whispered, his voice harsh and ragged. "All evening you'll feel my come in you and you'll remember me moving in you, filling you." He slid his hand further up and caressed her, slick and warm.

"When no one's looking, I'm going to take you around a corner and touch you like this and make you come." He bent his head to her neck as his finger explored her sheath. His voice was a mere breath against her skin. He could smell her sweet fragrance and the smell of sex. Other men would smell it, too, and he intended to make sure that there be no doubt about the man she'd had sex with. He pressed more deeply into her until he felt her sharp intake of breath and then a moan. "You won't think of anyone but me." His thumb circled her clitoris and he shuddered. "No one but me, Eve. No one."

She tugged sharply at his hair and he lifted his head. Her pupils were dilated and her hand trembled as she caressed his cheek.

"There *is* no one but you," she whispered.

THAT WAS SO HARD, Eve thought five hours later as she and Marcus stood outside his house.

She looked up at that hard, beloved face, drinking in his features. The event and the reception felt like they had lasted days. She bitterly resented having had to share him these past hours.

The reception had been so elegant, the theme *Winter Wonderland,* all in white. White tablecloths, giant white calla lilies everywhere, wreaths of white roses, all to celebrate a new literary festival. She'd been chosen to be the keynote speaker. An enormous honor, one that would have filled her with pride and pleasure a month ago, and had, when she'd accepted the honor.

But living so intensely with Marcus, secluded with him in his underground palace, had changed her forever. Every day he apologized for her having to stay with him. Every day he told her that in normal circumstances, he'd take her anywhere she wanted to go. To the finest restaurants. To first run movies. To all the most popular plays, including those for which tickets were impossible to find. He even said he wished he could hire a jet to take her to Aruba for a few days.

But her response was always the same—*I'm happy here with you.* His face always relaxed at her words.

Christmas had come and gone and they'd hardly noticed.

They hadn't needed the outside world at all. Both of them had been perfectly content to spend their time together watching videos, playing chess and going for a swim in his heated indoor pool as the snowflakes drifted past the window.

And making love, endlessly.

She remembered his hard words, and how shocked she'd been at them.

I want to make you scream with pleasure, over and over again. I want to fuck you so much your body will be molded to mine, your cunt shaped to my cock, your skin smelling of me. I want you to forget where you end and I begin.

It had been nothing less than the truth. Her body was so attuned to his, she couldn't begin to understand how she had lived without him. She was so happy they were back in their haven.

Eve shivered as Marcus put his palm to the scanner and the entrance door hissed open.

Snow had fallen all evening, but now the clouds had cleared and a million bright stars shone, remote and cold and beautiful. The deep mantle of snow reflected the light of the full moon, almost as bright as day.

They descended, Marcus's hand at her waist. He'd never been more than a handspan's distance from her all evening. She shifted and felt her nipples brush against the heavy silk of her evening jacket.

He'd been right. His lovemaking had sensitized

her body so much that she could hardly think of anything but being possessed by him. She felt him everywhere—her breasts, her belly, between her thighs.

She'd given her speech and, judging from the applause and the delighted looks of the organizers, she'd been successful. She had made literary small talk with two editors, a journalist-turned-book reviewer for the New York Times Book Review, a world-famous international publisher and the editor-in-chief of the local newspaper. They, too, had shown signs of interest in what she was saying, though she couldn't remember what had come out of her mouth. She didn't care about retro machismo or the structure of Jonathan Franzen's latest novel.

Not with Marcus brushing his hand down her arm, standing so close behind her she could feel his body heat, his arm around her waist.

The slightest sway brought her up against that powerfully muscled body. All it took was one glance out of heavy-lidded eyes and she could feel her body preparing itself for him. Her nipples beaded and she had to clench her thighs against the sharp desire, so sensitized by his love-making just moments before leaving the house that it was almost as if she could still feel him, hot and hard and deep inside her.

She'd found it impossible to concentrate on anything but him.

And everything that had been so very important to her before him was like ashes. The men all seemed so preposterous, jockeying for position, trying to impress everyone, constantly checking their status. Most of them carried on conversations looking over the shoulder of the person they were talking to, in case someone more important walked by. The women, too, with their surgically altered faces, some so Botoxed they could barely move their lips.

And not one, she was convinced, actually loved books. They loved best seller lists, and movies made from the books, and the publicity that surrounded bestsellers and they loved buzz. But they didn't love the books themselves.

She'd have felt incredibly lonely in the crowd if it hadn't been for Marcus, quietly standing behind her, observing and not talking. Just touching him made her feel less like an atom lost in space.

Before midnight, Marcus quietly suggested they leave and she'd agreed, relieved that the charade was finally over. She wasn't interested in talking to or being with anyone but Marcus.

There would be time enough in the future to have pleasant cocktail party conversations with her new acquaintances, but for now, she'd had enough.

Of everyone there tonight—the best and the brightest the city and the state could offer—the only one she'd really wanted to talk to was Marcus.

She wanted to know what he thought about the book she'd presented and its overly anxious author, she wanted to know whether he'd found the Senator's prissy wife as ridiculous as she did and whether he agreed that the champagne was too sweet.

Eve realized she could spend the rest of her life with only Marcus and be happy.

The elevator came to a halt, opened with a soft whoosh and Eve stepped out, Marcus right behind her. The first time she'd arrived, the house had seemed like something out of a fairy tale, unearthly and magical.

Now it felt like comfort and safety. It felt like home.

She turned, put her arms around Marcus's waist. He immediately embraced her. She sighed and burrowed against his shoulder. She didn't want a kiss she wanted this—this feeling of closeness, of connection.

"We're home," he said in his deep voice.

"Home," she sighed.

9

New Year's Eve

"**W**hat's happening?" Three days later, Marcus nudged her knee with his under the covers.

Eve put down her tablet and looked up with a smile. "Well, let me see. After the EMP took out the electricity grid, our stalwart group of survivors, led by a former Army Ranger, made it over the Rockies, trying to get to a survivalist stronghold. But they've been captured by a white supremacist group, the Sons of Freedom, who want to lynch the Ranger, kill the men and make the women sex slaves. The Ranger is ready to fight back." She tapped the screen of the tablet. "I imagine that by book 3 they'll have escaped and made it to the Stronghold. It's an exciting story, not particularly well written. You?"

Marcus shifted his pillows heaped against the leather headboard of the bed. "Hmm. So the male protagonist is a successful advertising executive in London. He's rich and healthy and depressed as hell. His wife left him because he was having an affair with his secretary and his teenage daughter hates him. He's an alcoholic and indulges a little too much in cocaine, wonders if he's an addict. He is. He is currently under the shower, hands against the wall, fully dressed in his Hugo Boss suit, contemplating suicide, but not before killing his evil, slimy boss. Depressing book, beautifully written, won the Booker last year."

"Hell is empty—" Eve said.

"And all the devils are here." Marcus finished for her.

"Well... not *here* here." Eve turned her head and kissed his shoulder.

He put his arm around her shoulders and kissed the side of her face. "No, not *here* here. Here, at this moment, it's sheer heaven."

Their eyes met.

"Extravagant words, but so very true."

They were. They'd been living in a bubble fashioned in heaven the past couple of days. Eve has lost track of how many days exactly had passed. Marcus had blackened the windows, put their cells face down and they entered a world without days and without time. She had no idea if it was even day or night. There was no staff, and all she knew was that at regular intervals, meals appeared, sprung from somewhere, like Athena from the forehead of Zeus.

Marcus appeared to have a bottomless freezer, so any time they got hungry, he would pull out pancakes and berries or eggplant parmesan or nasi goreng or a lemon cheesecake. They had no idea whether they were eating breakfast, lunch or dinner. He once asked her to express a wish and she'd said *boeuf bourguignon* laughingly and damned if a big serving bowl of—yep —boeuf bourguignon didn't appear on the table an hour later.

They didn't turn on the news or read the news. The outside world didn't impinge in any way—they didn't let it. They watched old movies cuddled up under a cashmere blanket on his fashionable but comfortable mile-long couch and binge-watched fantasy series. They made love, endlessly.

Recently, they'd discovered reading together and she didn't know whether that was her favorite activity with him. After the sex, of course. And the food.

But it was close.

Reading had always been her refuge against the world. To read *with* someone, who was on her wavelength...God. It was so delicious. Who knew?

She sighed. "I could do this forever." She stiffened and lifted her head from his shoulder. It was the first time she'd mentioned a future. It had just slipped out of her. "Sorry, I—"

He eased her head back onto his shoulder. "God, yes. Just stay here. Close the world right out. Just be together for the rest of our days and not even think of anything else."

There was a future that stretched out before them that was just like the present. Closed up in his super comfortable world, doing as they pleased, making love, eating, watching TV and reading. Without a schedule and without anyone telling them what to do and when to do it. Forever and ever. Maybe when spring came, they'd venture out for a walk, though Eve had no idea if there were nature walks possible around his place. All she'd seen was industrial wasteland.

No matter. She could happily stay exactly where she was till the end of time.

But there were black clouds far away on the horizon and worrying thoughts buzzing like gnats when she thought of the future. Because, well, she had a career. And she was going to have to pick it up at some point. She had meetings scheduled and talks with executives of the streaming company that employed her and writers to meet to see if they'd make good interview subjects. She'd already missed some meetings. She knew that. Her mind skittered away every time she thought of it. She could claim a devastating flu, but sooner or later...

"Don't worry about it, darling." Marcus nudged her shoulder with his. "Not now. Not yet."

She reared back and looked at him. At that dark, handsome face that in a short span of time had become so dear to her. When she'd first met him, in her father's study, she'd thought him a man of stone—completely emotionless. But he wasn't without feelings, he'd just learned to hide his feelings well. She was starting to be able to decipher the enigma that was Marcus Rey.

"So you're reading minds, now, eh?"

He smiled. "Not so hard to do when I can almost see the worries buzzing in your head. You're thinking about the future and—" His face froze, his entire body completely immobile. He cocked his head, eyes rolling toward the ceiling. Before she could ask what was wrong, he threw himself over her, completely covering her, in the instant that a huge booming sound filled the room and the roof fell in.

LIGHT. Darkness. Light. Darkness. Acrid smells. Something in the air that made it impossible to breath. No sounds. His ears had shut down.

Light. Darkness.

Pain.

Marcus pushed himself up on an elbow, trying to ignore the stabbing pain in his head, as if someone stuck a red-hot poker in his brain, and the burning pain on his right side. He looked down at the pillow which was soaked and red. Something else was red, pale human flesh ...

Eve!

Pure panic ate through his pain and disorientation. Eve was wounded! His

frantic hands ran over her but he couldn't see the source of blood. No rent skin, no gaping wounds. He lifted her shoulder to see if somehow she was wounded in her back, when she opened her eyes and stopped his hands with hers.

She blinked woozily. Her head wobbled a little as she focused on his face.

"Eve!" he shouted. "Are you hurt?"

Only the words didn't come out loud and strong. They came out garbled, a whisper. And his hands, patting her all over to see where she was wounded, were trembling and uncoordinated.

"Marcus." The ringing in his ears was too loud. He couldn't hear her voice, just followed her lips. She stilled his hands with her own. "I'm not hurt. You are."

She guided his hands to his head, where he winced as he felt a long open gash, bleeding heavily. Blood loss was okay, what made him frantic was this terrible weakness he felt.

Another boom, this time felt more by air displacement than sound, given his temporary deafness. Dust swirled in the air, making them cough. Another section of the roof fell in and the sky was exposed.

They were under attack! But from where? From inside? Marcus would have sworn that no one could break in. It looked like the attack came from above. Another boom, another section of roof collapsed, exposing the beams and struts of the superstructure.

Marcus knew how strong his home was. He'd gone over the plans with structural engineers and not just the architect. He wanted a hardened home, able to withstand an attack. Somehow, someone was raining missiles on them. But...how? From helicopters? His hearing was too shot to be certain, but he'd have felt the vibrations of a helicopter.

The next explosion was closer, and a beam crashed across the bed. A second before, instinct told him to grab Eve and roll with her to the floor.

He still couldn't think clearly but *protect Eve* was paramount in his mind, an incessant drumbeat. He looked down at her, at his beloved. She was ice white, streaks of blood down her cheeks where his bloodied hands had touched her. She looked scared but not panicked. Good girl.

What do we do? His hearing was coming back a little. Her voice sounded faraway but at least he could hear it, and read her lips.

He reached up to his bedside table and opened the drawer and took out a Glock 19 and his cell, which he'd switched to vibration. The Glock had a full magazine, he'd checked before putting it in the drawer because when you needed a weapon, chances were you needed it *now*. And you needed it ready to shoot.

He put a hand to the ground next to her head to lift himself up but crashed right down on top of Eve. Fuck! He didn't have the energy to lift his torso! He tried again, got halfway up, then his limbs trembled and he slumped back down. How the hell was he going to get them out of here if he couldn't even stand up?

A hand on his cheek. Eve, turning his face to her. She pointed at her eyes, the universal symbol for seeing, then jerked her thumb up. *We need to see what's going on.*

Marcus frowned.

Eve slowly stood up, still a little woozy but stable. He heard a faraway crash but couldn't figure out from which direction. Eve stepped away from the bed and in a panic, Marcus clutched her ankle.

"No!" Where was she going? He didn't know if the house was full of invaders. Eve looked down at his hand around her ankle and lifted his fingers, one by one. *Trust me,* she mouthed.

Ok. They were in a dangerous situation and he needed info now. He weighed options and realized she was right. He opened his hand reluctantly, and she walked carefully through the rubble to the doorway. He had to squint to focus and totally ignored the pain. A light fixture flickered, creating a strobe effect that bounced off the dust in the room. It looked like Eve was walking underwater.

Shaking, his head hurting so much with every movement he thought he would throw up, he managed to make it to his knees, steadied his hands clasped around the Glock on the bed and followed her movements, covering her.

Was he dying? Maybe he was. He'd never felt like this before, almost completely out of the world. He'd been shot once, but besides the pain, he'd felt exactly as he had before being shot. Now he felt like someone had propelled him into another dimension, where things jumped and wavered. Where time stretched and contracted. Where he felt like the floor could disappear under him at any moment.

Maybe it could. Something had blasted open his roof. Maybe it could blow up the floor. Maybe aliens had landed or monsters had come ravening up from the earth's core...

Whatever it was, he was going to protect Eve to his dying breath.

"Marcus!" Eve slid to her knees in front of him. She put her hand over his hands clasping the gun, jumping at the sound of another explosion. Rubble cascaded from the ceiling. "The roof has blown away! I could see sky in the huge hole gouged in the ceiling. There are these...things buzzing, I don't—"

She stopped, put a hand to her mouth.

"Drones," she whispered, just as he said, "Drones."

It was hard to put things together in his head, but he managed. Someone had sent drones to drop explosives over his home. *Petrov*. It could only be Petrov. Petrov wasn't coming back until tomorrow.

His home was under attack. Eve was under attack. In a burst of clarity, he realized what had to be done. He had two emergency exits. He needed to hustle Eve down to one of the two exits—probably the west exit —make it to a safe house. Gather his resources and counter-attack. He should have killed Petrov right away, right after Eve was attacked, instead of wallowing in pleasure with Eve. But it wasn't too late, he'd find out how to penetrate Petrov's defenses and go on the attack, after securing Eve. He should—

But then the clouds came back and he grasped at ideas like a blind man catching flies. He should... he should what? His head was spinning around, he couldn't focus in any way. Everything looked cloudy and dim, even his head was cloudy and dim. He tried an old trick from childhood when he despaired. Cut down the timeline to the next five minutes. Survive the next five minutes, then the next five and the next.

Okay, he thought, placing a hand on the floor, first

thing—stand up. He tried to rise but the world swirled around him and he started to collapse. But he couldn't because Eve lodged her shoulder under his arm and held him. He was heavy and he could feel her stagger, but she braced herself.

He was upright, but that was about it. He wiped blood from his eyes and shook his head.

"Marcus," Eve said and he slowly turned his head to look at her. She was scared, but steady. "I don't know what's happening, but we need to go."

Need to go. Need to go. The meaning of the words eluded him.

Something buzzed and they both looked at his bedside table. His cell, lit up and vibrating. Marcus reached out but missed, banging his hand on the corner. Eve picked his cell up.

"Hello?" She nodded. "Yeah. He's right here. But he's concussed, was hit by something, he's bleeding heavily. Speakerphone? Okay."

Eve fumbled with his cell's screen. Marcus wanted to help her, show her how to turn the speakerphone function on, but his fingers wouldn't obey him. His hands were trembling.

His legs wouldn't carry him and he sat heavily on the edge of the bed. Eve sat next to him.

"Ah!" Eve figured it out, put the phone between them. "We're both here."

"Sitrep!" the Major's deep voice barked.

Eve took the corner of the bedsheet and calmly cleaned Marcus's face as she spoke. Marcus opened his mouth but nothing came out.

"Marcus is unable to speak at the moment," Eve said. "From what I can see, we've been attacked from above. From drones, I think, carrying explosives. I don't know how many bombs were dropped, but the ceiling in the bedroom has partially collapsed and outside the bedroom, in the living room, the ceiling is gone. And—"

Another boom. Eve gave a cry and threw her body over his. In this through the looking glass world, Eve was trying to protect *him*! A chunk of ceiling thudded to the floor not two feet from them and debris rained down.

The Major was shouting over the cell. His voice faded in and out and Marcus couldn't make out what he was saying. Eve spoke to him and cut off the call.

She angled her head close to his. "Marcus." She shook his shoulder, hard. "Marcus listen to me! Marcus, wake up!" His eyes drifted shut. "Marcus, I need you!"

His eyes popped open.

"Marcus, the Major told me we had to get to the west exit. Do you know where that is? Nod if you understand me!"

His head jerked up and down.

Another loud boom, a little further off. The sound of falling masonry and shattered glass.

Eve had put her arms over his head, but now grabbed his hands. "My darling, I need you to try to stand and walk because I can't carry you. The Major said that he'll be waiting for us at the west exit with a vehicle and that you'd know why we had to escape from there."

Yes, the west exit...he'd planned escape routes with input from the Major. He'd know why they had to get to the west exit, if only there wasn't this dull black buzzing hole where that knowledge should be.

"You need to get up, Marcus. I need you to get up *now*! The Major said there were enough drones overhead to completely obliterate your home. It will take

time, but if we wait, we will die. Marcus, get up
please!"

Tears carved tracks in the dust on her face. She
looked like a mourning Madonna. She needed him. It
wasn't in him to deny her anything, not with that note
of desperation in her voice.

Eve tugged hard at his arms, crying and shouting.
She was like a radio signal tuning in and out. When he
could tune her in, he wanted with every cell in his
body to help her, to protect her. When she tuned out,
he was lost in a dark forest with monstrous creatures,
unable to fight his way out.

He tuned her in. "Eve?" he croaked.

"Thank God!" Eve sniffed, wiped at her cheeks,
tears spreading the dirt. "Marcus, we need to get out,
we need to get to the west exit. The Major said he'd
meet us there, because we can't stay here. The entire
place is being destroyed. Get up my darling, please
get up!"

Marcus understood just a few words, *west exit* and
get up. He placed his hands on his knees, squared his
shoulders.

"Yes, darling, now stand!" Eve was crying freely
now but she was at his side, tugging his arm upwards.
She wanted him to stand up. Eve needed him to stand
up. He heaved with all his strength and stood, swaying. Eve's arm went around his back and she stopped
him from falling on his ass. He looked at her, her
strength and desperation. She needed him.

He staggered, kept himself from falling by taking a
step forward. Another. Trembling. Another explosion,
closer this time. He didn't quite understand what was
happening but explosions close to Eve were bad. Instinctively, he headed away from the explosion.

Suddenly, Eve stopped and looked down. What?

The explosions were coming from up. She frowned at the floor and he followed her gaze. The corridor had flooring of a light neutral gray. Not red. Where did the red come from? A drop of red fell, another. From him. It was coming from him.

And now pain came roaring in, masked up until now by adrenaline and the pain of the concussion. He lifted the black sweatshirt that was glistening and saw a metallic shard sticking out of his side. He had no idea if it had nicked an artery but there was a hell of a lot of blood.

"Marcus!" Eve's horrified voice penetrated the darkness in his head. She turned and whipped a runner off a side table, then stood, hesitating. There was no way to staunch the bleeding without either pulling the shard out or pushing it further in. Her hands, crimson with his blood, shook, an inch from his flesh. She looked up at him, anguished.

Another boom, even closer.

He grabbed Eve's hand, slippery with his blood.

"Eve." He had trouble focusing, breathing. "You have to go now. West. Exit."

Then weakness took him and he slid to his knees.

10

"**Y**ou have to go," Marcus said. "West. Exit." His voice was weak now, his breathing labored. He grunted in pain when she tried to wipe the blood away from the shard of metal in his side. Beads of sweat appeared on his face.

He teetered and fell to his knees.

"Leave you? Are you crazy?" Eve took his hands and her heart gave a lurch. They were stone cold. Marcus, whose body was a furnace. "Come on, stand up," she said. "You can do it." She kneeled next to him to fit her shoulder under his arm. Tears ran down her face and she wiped them on his sleeve. "Come on, darling. Get up."

Marcus didn't budge. Slowly, he reached into his pocket, grimacing with pain. He pulled out a gun and pressed it into her hand. He curled her hand around the stock.

"That's a Glock 19, Eve. It's a semi-automatic. All you need to do is aim and keep pulling the trigger. You'll feel a break in the trigger, which is the safety. Keep pulling. It's ready to shoot."

Eve opened her mouth and he put a finger across

her lips, leaving bloody stains. His eyes bored into hers, willing her to pay attention.

"Leave me. Go. Now. The Major is waiting for you."

Eve held Marcus's face still with both hands, so he was forced to look at her. He was fading fast, but he needed to hear this.

"I will not leave you. If you don't come with me, then we are both going to die here." She jumped as another explosion filled the hallway with dust. They both coughed, and Marcus's wound bled more heavily. "You must come with me."

His face was frozen with pain and regret. "No—"

She held up a finger as his cell rang. M. For Major, she assumed.

A deep, angry voice barked, "The fuck are you, Marcus? I see you as still in the building. More drones are coming. Get the fuck out!"

"It's Eve," she answered. "Marcus has been wounded. He can barely stand and he's losing blood. I'm going to try to get us to you, but I don't know where the west exit is."

Silence. Then: "Marcus would want you to leave him and save yourself."

"Not going to happen. Give me another option."

He growled, "You're outside the master bedroom, right?"

"Yep. In that big corridor."

"Okay, follow that to the end. At the end of the passageway is a keypad. The code is 1991. Go through the doors and turn right. I'm coming to get you. Try to get as far as you can with Marcus."

Eve felt her throat constrict. "If he falls, I can't pick him up and I can't carry him and we'll both die. Please hurry."

"On my way." The connection closed.

Eve studied Marcus. She had meant every word. She wasn't leaving without him. But it was going to be hard.

He was sweating profusely now, lines of pain bracketing that beautiful mouth. Eve studied his face, the face of the man she loved. She'd never thought to have love, but now she'd found it. Marcus was the greatest miracle of her life.

No way was she going to lose him.

Move fast. An explosion went off thirty feet down the corridor. Marcus's head came up. Though his face was pinched and gray, his gaze was suddenly sharp and aware.

He reached out with his big hand and caressed her face, leaving a bloody trail. "God, I... love you."

"I know, darling." Eve managed to get the words out past the huge lump in her throat.

"Go now, Eve." His voice was a mere whisper.

"Marcus," she said. "You're going to die."

He nodded and closed his eyes.

"And I'm going to die, too."

His eyes snapped open again. "No!" he croaked. "Get out of here!"

"Both of us are going to die, and then we're going to live again. Somewhere far away. We're going to start a new life together somewhere else, where no one knows who we are. We're going to leave our past behind us. But first you've got to get up, Marcus." Eve placed his arm around her shoulders, her own arm went around his waist. "Help me here."

He shook his head.

"Marcus," she whispered. "*Please*. I'm not leaving here without you."

His eyes looked intently into hers and she knew he

could read the truth of what she said. She wasn't leaving without him.

He gritted his teeth and Eve gave up a silent prayer of thanks as he staggered forward. One step. Two.

She stared down the long, dark corridor. It looked a hundred miles long.

Another explosion.

Marcus staggered and Eve braced herself against the wall. "Marcus,

Please," she whispered. "We have to make it out together. If you love me,

Marcus...*move!*"

Marcus lurched forward and Eve half-carried, half-dragged him down the corridor.

Eve shuffled forward as fast as she could. Marcus's arm was heavy around her shoulders and she bore most of his weight. She didn't know how long she could last but was grimly determined to take him with her or die in this corridor.

"Put your left foot forward, Marcus, then your right. That's wonderful, you can do this, darling. You're the strongest man I've ever met. Did I ever get a chance to tell you how much I love you?" She sneaked a glance up and saw his lips curve faintly in his pale face. He shook his head.

"I didn't think so. Keep moving, Marcus, you can do it. This guy, this Major, is going to meet us at the west exit, whatever that is."

She kept talking, hoping to distract him. He shuffled along like an old man, barely lifting his feet. The corridor stretched before them, dimly lit with a few wall sconces. She had no idea how long this passage would go on. However long, though, they would walk it.

"My best friend in college went on to get a degree

in medicine, did you know that? She lives about twenty miles from here." Marcus's eyes were closed. "Open your eyes, Marcus and listen to me."

He looked down at her, eyes slightly glazed. She shook him and he swayed. It was terrifying to see a man as powerful and vital as Marcus look so weak. "Listen to me, damn it. Listen. We're going to live. We're going to go to my friend and she'll take care of that wound and I'll take care of you until you recover. And then you're going to get us some false documents and we'll get out of the country. But right now, my darling, I need for you to walk out of this place. I need you to help me. Can you do that? I love you so much and I don't want to live if you die and I need you to help me *now*. Can you do that?"

"Yes."

Eve closed her eyes in relief. His voice was weak, barely a croak, but she heard his determination. She had no idea where he found the energy, what depths of reserves he had to dip into, but miraculously, he straightened.

She nearly gasped in relief as some of the pressure lifted from her shoulders. She hurried them as fast as she dared. Marcus staggered but was upright.

The nightmare trip seemed to take hours. She dripped with sweat and Marcus swayed on his feet when she finally saw the steel door at the end of the corridor.

Wheezing, she leaned against the corridor wall for a moment, allowing her screaming muscles a chance to rest, then pushed away again.

From behind them came the sound of another explosion. Eve felt the heat and the rush of air. She punched the numbers into the key pad and pushed Marcus out the door. They were wherever they were supposed to be going. When the door opened, a huge man rushed in. Blond and blue-eyed, but with Marcus's strong build and just as tough-looking. Actually, he looked mean, and if she didn't know he was loyal to Marcus, she would never have trusted him.

"Major?"

"Yeah. Give him here, you look like you're about to faint."

His voice was deep and rough. Eve had zero choices. She eased herself from under Marcus's shoulder and allowed this man to lean forward and position Marcus in a fireman's carry. He shouldered Marcus's massive weight with a grunt and immediately took the right-hand corridor. He was fast, even carrying Marcus. Eve scrambled to keep up. She wasn't going to let Marcus out of her sight.

"Fuckers used drones." That deep voice was furious. "Didn't see that coming at all, but that will never happen again. Fuckers also got two of my men. *That* won't happen again, either."

Eve didn't care about his professional pride or his lost men. All she cared about was not losing Marcus. "I have a friend who is a doctor who lives not far from here. We can—"

"No." He looked down at her, his mouth grim. "Marcus needs surgery and a clinic." She opened her mouth to protest, knowing Marcus would want to keep a low profile. "Don't worry. No one will be reporting it to the police and no one will know it's him. I'll get him in with an alias and I'll have four men in rotation at all times. He'll be safe."

He'd better be, she thought.

A few minutes later, they were at the end of the corridor and an SUV was there. Big, black, undoubtedly armored and probably bristling with weapons. Not far away was the mouth of a tunnel.

"Drones will be watching for our escape, but this tunnel goes on for five miles. When we exit, no one can tell where we came from. And my men are providing diversions."

He motioned for her to get into the back seat and she scrambled across the seat, back to the door. The Major gently set Marcus down until his head was in her lap. He was boneless, unconscious. In a sudden spurt of panic, Eve put a finger to the side of his neck and felt his pulse—weak and thready. The Major took a foil blanket from the storage area at the back and covered Marcus.

"Hurry," Eve whispered, terrified as she looked at the still features of the man she loved.

"You got it." The Major gunned the engine and they aimed right at the tunnel, back tires sliding a little on the gravel.

A fiery cloud rose up into the night sky, followed by smoke billowing up. Marcus's beautiful home, his sanctuary, was burning to the ground.

Eve took her eyes off Marcus to look ahead at the mouth of the tunnel and was astonished to see an explosion on the horizon, ahead of her instead of behind her. She wondered if she was hallucinating, then recognized the stars and pinwheels and brightly colored bursts of joyful light.

Fireworks.

It was midnight.

The new year had begun.

EPILOGUE

LA VALLETTA, MALTA: 3 YEARS LATER

"Hi honey, I'm home!" Jacob Hudson's deep voice floated into the kitchen from the cavernous entry. It was their inside joke. He worked in his sumptuous study on the second floor and his commute consisted of walking down the curving stone staircase. A ten second commute, if that.

Nova Hudson smiled. She'd just set the table. They had a remarkable cook who came in at 10 a.m. and left at one, leaving magic behind. "What remarkable timing. We're ready for lunch. Just in time. How did you know that lunch was ready?"

"Smelled it." Her husband caught her around the waist and twirled with her in his arms. "Miriam cooked fish, right?"

"Two sea bream, freshly caught this morning. Grated carrot and beetroot salad with feta cheese. Baked figs, the figs from our fig tree. That wine from Crete we love. We're going to live forever."

He threw back his head and laughed. Marcus Rey had never laughed, but Jacob Hudson, well...he laughed and smiled often. Come to think of it, she did too. It was why she'd chosen the name Nova. She felt like a brand-new woman. She *was* a brand-new woman.

Jacob and Nova Hudson. Americans, one of Maltese stock, who'd chosen to make their lives in the crowded, sun-drenched Mediterranean island of Malta. In La Valletta, though the truth was that the city *was* the island.

They'd talked it over, where to hide. Researched areas that were deserted and remote. They'd been ready to become New Zealanders, living in Haast, with the closest supermarket two hours away. Or Iceland, the northernmost part of the West Fjords. Greenland. Tierra del Fuego. The Shetland Islands. If it was remote, they'd studied it.

But the places felt unwelcoming. And *cold*. It had been a long cold winter in their city and cold held no appeal. They had been idly looking at luxury real estate and came across Palazzo Paradiso in La Valletta. At the same time, they realized that being in a crowded place might be safer than in a remote place.

Malta. One of the most densely populated places on earth. Palazzo Paradiso. The name alone... It was a 17th century palazzo right on the coast, in the northern part of the city. It needed some cosmetic work, but not that much. *Some good face creams,* Nova had said, *but not plastic surgery.*

In the carousel of photos showing sundrenched golden stone walls, arched doorways, a beautiful curving stone staircase with a broken balustrade, you could see the bones of the beauty she'd been. And then they'd seen the courtyard. The entire palazzo curled around it in a protective golden embrace. What looked like an acre—even accounting for a wide-angle lens—of terracotta tiling of a hidden gem of an immense courtyard, one side looking out over the blue,

blue sea. The huge terrace had trellises of wisteria and grapes.

They both fell in love immediately. Marcus contacted a man he knew who provided them with impeccable identities and reached deep into the bowels of the Maltese government and plucked a Maltese maternal grandfather who immigrated to the United States in 1961 out of thin air. Marcus became Jacob Hudson, with an automatic claim to citizenship, which was expedited thanks to a one-off payment of $100,000. As the wife of a citizen of Malta, Nova, qualified for citizenship, too.

She automatically thought of them as Jacob and Nova, now.

Palazzo Paradiso had proved easy and fun to restore. The building was sound, it just needed updates. It wasn't huge. They didn't need a lot of space. It was just perfect.

Two months after landing, Jacob had bought a shipping company that was responsible for three quarters of the passengers and goods coming to and from Malta. They had been careful in setting up their new identities, but he'd also been very careful when buying the company. He was not on record as the owner, just shell company after shell company. The last shell company nominated Jacob Hudson as CEO. He learned the ropes fast and ran the company well.

Jacob employed top flight people, paid them above the going rate, and turned it into a highly successful company. He often said he enjoyed this job infinitely more than moving money around, which is what he had been doing back in the States. He had a fortune Jorge had set aside for him, but he didn't touch it. They lived simply and Argos Shipping more than kept them in style.

Plus she now had her own income, which was a problem. Jacob knew nothing about it.

Jacob put a heavy arm around her shoulders and squeezed gently. She loved it when he did that. Even after three years, it still made her feel protected and grounded. He bent to kiss the side of her face. She closed her eyes and inhaled his scent. Lemon soap, sandalwood shampoo, and man.

"Where are we having lunch, honey?" he asked, nipping her ear.

She shivered, drew in a deep breath. "I set the table out on the terrace. It's warm enough." It was December but Malta was blessed with a warm climate. Year round. They both loved it.

"Great." He smiled down at her as he steered them out onto the terrace. He stopped on the threshold of the big French windows giving out onto the terrace. His arm tightened around her shoulders and he sighed.

Yeah. It was a pretty sight. The table was set under the thickest branch of wisteria, close to the low stone parapet looking out over the sea. Vividly colored flowers in pots brightened the perimeter and one wall was covered in purple bougainvillea.

The sun was bright, casting little golden waves on the blue sea. Something big moved along the horizon. The 12:15 Argos Shipping Ferry from La Valletta to Athens, making its way east. Four sailboats sliced across the water. Several fishing boats were visible on the horizon. It was entirely likely that they would eat two of those fish tomorrow.

The table was long and Nova had used one of the many hand-embroidered linen tablecloths she'd found in the Saturday market here. The plates were earthenware in bright swirls of cobalt blue and cream fashioned by a ceramicist she'd made friends with. Cut flowers from their garden were in a glass vase, a riot of colors against the white linen. There was a crystal pitcher of the superb Greek wine that came in on Jacob's ferries.

"I can't believe we get to live this way," she whispered and he dropped another kiss on the top of her head.

"Yeah." He shot her a glance. "Beats before."

She sighed and smiled. "God yes. It certainly does." Neither of them missed their old life. In the three years since they'd disappeared, they'd slowly relaxed, in stages.

Stage one. A fancy clinic, where Marcus underwent a four-hour surgery and required massive blood transfusions. Over five days, he recovered in a private room and Eve never left his side. Four men, in rotation, sat outside the room and no one in the clinic said anything.

The Major was really pissed. At himself, most of all. He couldn't forgive himself for not anticipating the drones. He was even more pissed when he discovered that it was one of his men, a new recruit, who had betrayed them. Had given Andrei Petrov the coordinates to Jacob's headquarters, which was why Petrov came back a day early from Mexico. The Major angrily paced the corridor outside Marcus's hospital room. Eve felt sorry for anyone who would make an attempt on their lives.

Every day, Marcus grew stronger and stronger. Eve could hardly believe it. He'd almost died and four days later he was shuffling down the hospital corridor.

The next stage was Santa Fe, a shelter for battered women. Eve had interviewed one of the founders of a sort of underground railroad for battered women.

She'd also donated a check for $10,000 because she believed in what the woman was doing. When she called in a favor, she found the warmest possible welcome.

Two of the Major's men drove them a day and a night and she had almost collapsed on the shelter's doorstep. Inside, she and Marcus found medical care and shelter for as long as they needed it.

But Marcus was strong and, as he told her afterwards, he had something to live for. His love for her had carried him through. He was ready to move on in a few days.

Stage Three. In the meantime, Jorge had been busy hiding their tracks, shifting money abroad and renting them a luxury penthouse condo in a building on the upper West Side of Manhattan. When Marcus was strong enough, a limo had appeared with two combat drivers recruited from the Major's company.

Their bodies were not found and Petrov was convinced they were still alive. Word on the street was that he had offered a million dollar bounty to anyone who provided info on their whereabouts and two million dollars to whoever killed them and brought him their heads. He was explicit. He wanted their heads, separated from their bodies, in a cooler bag.

It was why they agreed to never have children. Both of them shuddered at the thought of a child of theirs in constant danger.

They hid out in Manhattan under temporary identities while Marcus recovered fully. She was fine with not going out. When they did go outside the apartment, no one paid them the slightest bit of attention. But Marcus knew that Andrei Petrov had contacts with members of the Russian mob based in Brighton Beach. Manhattan was a short drive away.

Once, walking along Fifth Avenue, Marcus thought he saw Petrov's second in command reflected in a store window. He bundled her into the store and bustled her right out the back. A quick phone call and one of the Major's men drove an armored car right up to the exit door in the back of the store. They drove straight to the underground garage where another one of the Major's men was waiting for them, armed and ready. They rushed to the elevator that went all the way to the penthouse without stopping and Marcus drew his first clear breath once the armored door closed behind them with the sound of a bank vault closing.

"That's it," he told her. "We're going abroad."

Stage four.

They looked at everything. Canada was too close and too cold. England had five million CCTV cameras. And further afield—Australia, New Zealand, South Africa. Nothing really appealed. Then they came across that listing for Palazzo Paradiso in La Valletta and everything fell into place.

Malta's official language was Maltese but everyone spoke English. It was dense and crowded, full of foreigners and tourists and no one paid them any attention at all.

They became Jacob and Nova Hudson.

The Major sent two of his men to accompany them to Malta and to stay with them, at his expense, and when two years had gone by without incident, he called them home. But they had grown fond of La Valletta. One was engaged to a dark-eyed beauty who ran a small restaurant. Jacob offered them jobs running security for Argos Shipping and they accepted with alacrity.

It was also clear that, if the need arose, they were

first and foremost Jacob and Nova's personal bodyguards.

They were safe. Except for Nova's little project which might have endangered them.

A perfect life and her selfishness might have put them in peril. She stared at her plate made by her good friend Caterina Bartolo. So beautiful, the swirls of color. Caterina was making her matching glasses and water and wine pitchers. She had an appointment the day after tomorrow to go antiquing with Caterina, who had a superb eye for antiques and the haggling skills of a carpet merchant in Marrakech.

If they had to run, she might never see Caterina again. They might have to abandon Palazzo Paradiso, which they had so lovingly restored. Jacob's company, which he took such pride in—abandoned. It didn't bear thinking about. And all because of her and her foolish what? Pride? Ego?

The fish had been carefully deboned, but Nova felt like she had fish bones stuck all the way down her gullet. She moved the food around her plate, hoping Jacob wouldn't notice. But, of course, he did.

When he'd finished his fish, he sat back and put his hand over hers, stilling the movements of the fork. "You know," he said gently, "the fish is excellent. And it should be going into your mouth instead of being shunted around the plate."

She raised her eyes to his. So dark and so knowing. She quickly looked back down at her plate.

"What's wrong, darling?" Oh God. His deep voice was soft, gentle, loving. Would it still be loving when he found out what she'd done? When he discovered that her selfishness might cost them their wonderful life? Because if they had to run again, she didn't think they could replicate what they'd found here. It was a one-off.

It felt like stones rattled in her chest and her heart beat against her ribs. He ran a big finger along her neck. Right where the blood ran. "Your heart is beating so fast, my love. Tell me what's wrong."

"Jacob," she whispered, voice raw. "I—" and her voice deserted her. The words simply would not come. Her entire chest was hot and painful. "I'm so sorry."

His dark eyebrows drew together. "You've done something?"

She couldn't speak and nodded.

"Something...bad?"

She nodded again.

He sat back, eyes carefully watching her face. "How bad? On a scale of one to ten."

"A hundred," she croaked.

"Hmm." He cocked his head, studying her. "That's pretty bad. So what could it possibly be? Did you spend all our money on the horses?"

If anything, she was guilty of earning too much money. She shook her head.

"Well, that's a relief. Did you break any Maltese laws and the *Policia* are going to break our front door down any minute?"

She shook her head again.

He sighed gustily and she looked at him narrow-eyed. Was he enjoying himself? A big grin showed that he was.

"It's not funny," she muttered.

"Darling, I beg to differ. The idea of you doing something really bad is vastly amusing. What did you do?"

It was too hard to explain. She pulled out her

tablet and went to a big ebook store. She found a book page and showed it to him. He studied it.

"*A Breath of Magic* by A. B. Carsons." He read the book blurb. "Okay. A fantasy novel, looks dark and exciting. Sort of like the books you like to read." He studied her face. "What am I looking at, besides a book that three thousand people have reviewed and liked?"

"Go down and see the ranking."

He obediently scrolled down. When he got to the ranking his eyebrows rose. "Huh. Number one bestseller. Good for A. B. Carsons, whoever he is."

"She."

"I beg your pardon?"

"Whoever she is."

"Okay. Whoever she is. So, who is she?"

"Me. She is me." Her heart swelled at what she'd done. A tear rolled down her cheek. "Me. I've ruined everything."

He hadn't heard her. He shot to his feet, pulled her up and hugged her hard. "You? You're the bestseller? Congratulations! I had no idea you were writing a book! Why didn't you tell me?"

"I...I was sort of embarrassed. Didn't think I could do it."

Nova had always wanted to write, had kept it a little secret inside her heart. She'd never tried an actual novel. She'd written hundreds of short stories, character studies, outlines of possible books. It was why she had such a rapport with writers. She understood them, down to the bone. But all those years scribbling had somehow prepared her for the day she settled down to seriously write.

The day she began was crystal clear in her memory. Another glorious day in Malta, Jacob was off for two days in Athens negotiating the purchase of a cargo ship. She had just finished decorating her study on the top floor. She'd opened her laptop for the first time in a year and the words came pouring out. A novel that had been in her heart for so many years. A young girl on a far-off planet under a cruel overlord, unaware of her own power. She wrote the first draft in under three months, hiding it from Jacob. He was guaranteed to tell her it was the best thing since Shakespeare because he loved her. But she wasn't sure how good it was. That instinctive ability to appreciate good writing in others deserted her. She had no idea whether it was any good or not.

She wrote and rewrote and rewrote and when she could rewrite no more, she finally commissioned a book cover from a young artist she admired, giving a fake name and paying via bank transfer from a bank account she opened up under another name. Then she uploaded it to all the ebook platforms, expecting absolutely nothing. She'd scratched an itch that had been bothering her for years and that was that.

Until the book was discovered by an enthusiastic reader, then ten, then a hundred, then a thousand and it just... took off. She'd watched it climb the charts with dismay. It wasn't supposed to be a success. It was just supposed to be something on her bucket list that she'd crossed off.

Jacob pulled away and looked down at her. "You're still frowning. How is this not a good thing, my best-selling wife?"

"Oh God. I just painted a huge bullseye on our backs! People pay attention to bestsellers! And so, they'll pay attention to me. To us. Our new life will be over. Oh Jacob, I'm so sorry!"

Another tear slipped down. Instead of wiping it

with his thumb, Jacob bent and licked it away. "Hush darling. You wrote it under a pen name, right?"

She nodded, biting her lips. She didn't dare open her mouth. She was afraid her sorrow would come out in a howl. She'd hoped to please a few readers and that no one would pay her any attention at all. She'd been so foolish and had put their wonderful new life in jeopardy. And for what?

"Well, if I understand the book market, you're going to have to open up some social media accounts in the name of A. B. Carson, right?"

Her breath came out in a huff of regret. "Yeah."

"That's easy enough. The photo on the Facebook page and on Instagram and Booktok can be one of those coy ones with a hank of hair and half an eye. Or from the back of your head, wearing a wig. Or a cartoon version of someone who doesn't look like you."

The panic was easing a little. Jacob sounded so reasonable. He wasn't panicking at all. He sounded like he had a plan. It wasn't a feasible plan but a plan, however flawed, was better than no plan at all. Which is what she had. Her mind had been a blank wall of panic since she'd seen that little #1 bestseller flag this morning.

"I don't think that will work for long. Fans can get a little avaricious. They want to know everything about an author and her life. They are going to want photos. And number of pets. And favorite recipes."

"Not if they knew how badly you cooked," Jacob said solemnly, startling a laugh out of her. She thought she'd never laugh again.

"But—" she began.

Jacob overrode her. "A. B. Carson is a pen name. The author behind the name suffers from acute social anxiety. Crippling social anxiety. It would be crass, not to mention politically incorrect, to force her out into the open. We can write one of those fake bios. A. B. Carson lives with her pet tarantulas on a faraway planet. Or else—A. B. Carson lives in a cave in Iceland with the Abominable Snowman. All the social media platforms can be filled with content that pertains only to the books—because my darling, you are going to write more books. The platforms will contain no personal information at all. I can set up a publishing house for you with a corporate structure no one can trace back to you. In fact, you've often said you wished you could publish promising young writers. You could do it all via email, all behind a VPN. The money you are earning can go into a US based bank account in the name of the publishing house then go straight to an off shore account. Some could be automatically streamed to that literacy program you liked. Remember?"

Reading for Fun. Established by a group of university students studying urban sociology, it gave out e-readers and scoured the platforms for bargain books and filled the e-readers with cheap but good reads. The kids loved the program.

"You're not mad at me," she whispered.

Something in his face changed, a ripple of...something...moved over his harsh features.

"Mad? Mad at you? For writing a good book? Am I insane?" Her imperturbable husband, who rarely showed emotions unless they were making love, looked indignant and a little hurt.

Nova winced. "I put us in danger. I could have exposed us. We could have lost everything, simply because of my ego. We still might lose everything, our wonderful life here."

"No, darling. You didn't put us in danger. You didn't

expose us. And we're definitely not going to lose everything. What am I here for?" He pointed at himself. "Not just a pretty face, you know. If I can hide us here, hide an entire palazzo and shipping company, I can wipe away the traces of the author of a book, no matter how good that book is. No, the only effect is that you've found you are good at something you've wanted to do your entire life and a few charities are going to get some unexpected funding. Win-win."

A flush of happiness shot through her, so welcome after the chill dread of the past few days. She'd been watching her book rise through the ranks like a helium balloon, unable to celebrate. It had been totally unexpected, that rise. The most she'd hoped for was a little following of enthusiastic readers, not this tsunami.

She blew out a breath, feeling her heart rate slow down.

"Don't tell me you've been worried," Jacob said, rearing back. "You're smart, my darling. Smarter than I am. This isn't like you, to be so dumb."

Dumb? He was calling her *dumb*?

"I had every right to be worried," she said heatedly. "It's not dumb to worry that two people on the run might suddenly have a spotlight of attention placed on them, which is what ate at me."

He smiled and she realized he'd deliberately provoked her, goading her into a heated response, when she'd felt so cold with dread.

Nova sat back. Blood was flowing back to her hands and feet, she was able to take in her surroundings. Panic was a brutal beast, robbing you of everything good in life.

"So this is what we're going to do."

Jacob took her hand, brought it to his mouth,

kissed it. His mouth, his breath were so warm. She was infused with heat and love.

"You're going to write some Facebook and Instagram posts, with photos from a very cold and arid place. The posts will be observations, studded with notes on how happy you are to be alone. How you suffer from anxiety and panic attacks. Maybe you'll have a dog." He angled his head, studying her. "No. A. B. Carson will have a cat. A cantankerous feral cat that hisses when you feed it. Carson likes that. She likes the thought of the cat not being attached to her. And you'll post them from an IP that cannot be traced. And you'll concoct a little automated response to fan mail essentially saying thank you for writing but don't do that again."

She could see it. See how an aura of misanthropy and neurosis could keep her safe. "After a while people won't write."

"Voilà." Jacob reached out a big hand and wiped away the frown between her eyebrows with his thumb. "Exactly what you want. *But* they'll keep buying your books."

She gave a startled laugh that surprised her. She never thought she'd be able to laugh about this. In the middle of the night she'd worried so much about being too big a success, about the two of them being tracked down, their identities exposed, giving up their new life. It was like having broken glass in her head.

"And any enterprising journalist trying to find out more about you will find a wall of ice from your publisher, which will be dedicated to maintaining your privacy. If J. D. Salinger can do it, so can you."

Nova turned and looked at her husband. At that hard, handsome face. At the breadth of his shoulders that could seemingly bear any burden.

They hadn't married officially, but that first night they slept on sleeping bags on the floor of the Palazzo they'd purchased sight unseen, Jacob had produced two beautiful claddagh rings in white and yellow gold, though he didn't have a drop of Irish blood in him. He liked the story of claddagh rings, two clasped hands around a heart, representing eternal love. Standing on the moonlit terrace, they'd taken vows to love and protect each other for the rest of their days and they were as married as any two people could be.

Jacob kept his vows and loved and protected her every second of every day.

He was protecting her now.

"Thank you, darling," she whispered. Her throat was tight with emotion.

He smiled again and bent to kiss her, a brush of lips that warmed her. "My pleasure. And I want to see more books, as many as you can write."

Nova shivered. Oh God. A lifetime living in this beautiful place, with the man she loved beyond reckoning, writing her books, the ones that had been living inside her all her life...it was almost too much happiness for one lifetime.

Jacob's gaze circled her face. He was a perceptive man, and where she was concerned, she felt like he could read, could almost feel, every emotion going through her. He could see how moved she was, how raw and emotional she was.

He bent to kiss her lightly again, picked up his fork. "Come on, this bream isn't going to eat itself."

It shattered that tight knot of emotions. It was a gorgeous day on their terrace, under the wisteria, with the smells of the sea and the freshly grilled fish making a kind of unique perfume that assailed the senses.

Nova felt light, as if an anvil had been lifted from her chest. The first forkful of the bream was delicious. She was spearing a second forkful when Jacob's cell rang. The refrain of *Highway to Hell*, Jorge's ringtone.

They both sobered at once. Jorge rarely called. He usually emailed over *Protonmail*, super secure, and he added the few details of his personal life he wanted to share when he sent Jacob his financial reports. Jacob skipped over the financial news, knowing Jorge had everything in hand, but always read the personal news.

It was 3 a.m. in Los Angeles, which is where Jorge had relocated, together with the latest boyfriend.

Not too much good news at 3 a.m.

Jacob slid his thumb over the screen and said simply, "Talk."

He listened and suddenly his eyes grew wide. Jacob never showed emotion when receiving news, but this time something important had happened.

"Wait," he said. "I'll put you on speakerphone."

He placed his cell on the table between them. His hand was trembling. Oh God. She didn't even know Jacob's hand *could* tremble. What on earth could make Jacob Hudson's hand tremble?

Please, please God, let it not endanger their lives here. But what else could shake Jacob if not abandoning their lives, maybe even overnight like they had back home? They both loved it here, were putting down roots, each day bringing new pleasures.

Minutes ago, she thought *she* had brought danger to their door, forcing them to go on the run. Jacob had laughed at her, but if it turned out they had to run, she had no doubt he'd have made excellent plans already, capable of changing on the fly if necessary, and would have taken them to the fallback position he undoubtedly had ready, without a cross word to her.

They were in this together, even if they had to jump ship and swim to another safe haven.

Her heart contracted at the thought. But she couldn't let Jacob see her distress. He'd done everything possible to keep them safe but sometimes fate gate-crashed and ruined the party.

So, she folded her hands in her lap and prepared herself for the worst. She'd been waiting three years to get devastating news. A minute in, her jaw dropped. She leaned forward, not believing her ears.

"Can you repeat what you said, Jorge?"

"You're sitting down, right?" Jorge's voice had a vein of excitement running through it. On the screen his dark eyes were bright and he almost quivered with emotion.

"On the chair I sanded myself," she assured him. She reached out blindly, finding Jacob's hand. Knowing she'd always find Jacob's hand ready for hers. His hand was warm, strong, grounding. Whatever was coming, they'd face it together.

"So, back home there was a shootout last night. Police are spare with the details, but Petrov was killed immediately. All the top members of his organization were killed. Essentially his Bratva is no more. Officially no one knows who did it, but unofficially, it was a hostile takeover by a new Russian gang, who are ambitious and ruthless and have already won the war, with a ferocious coup in the night. Like the last scene of The Godfather on steroids. The leader, Dmitri Nikitin, has already established his men in all the top positions Petrov occupied. It's like Petrov was never there."

On the screen, a broadly grinning Jorge held up a finger. "But," he said and paused dramatically.

Nova leaned forward.

Jacob rolled his eyes. "Cut to the chase, Jorge."

"But..." he repeated in dramatic tones, patting the air as if to say, *wait*. "There's more. I reached out delicately and touched Nikitin and enquired about you. Talked to his top lieutenant and then talked to the Big Man himself. They didn't actually know who you are. Then the top lieutenant remembered Petrov had a vendetta against you, but as far as he's concerned, that was years ago, and ancient history. Could have been the Peloponnesian War, for all he cares. You are not a factor in his calculations at all. The whole thing has been cut off and buried. No one is coming after you, ever again. The two of you are safe."

At the word 'safe', Nova gave a deep sob and her eyes filled with tears. Something pulsed painfully in her chest.

Safe.

She and Jacob had never been safe. And now they were. Safe to live out their beautiful, low-key lives to the end of their days. Enjoy each other, their golden stone home, their new friends. Get to the spend the rest of their lives together in the open, like normal people did.

It was an immense gift, one she had never expected to receive, dropped in their lap.

Jorge pulled back when he saw Nova's tears. Tears alarmed him. He addressed Jacob. "Hey man, I'm sending you the police reports and the news reports and newscast clips. Plus some emails scraped from the new Bratva. You are never mentioned, not once." His eyes slid to Nova, next to Jacob, unmoving, tears streaming down her face. "Gotta run, will be sending you more news. But it will all confirm what I'm telling you. You're clear. You're safe. Enjoy the rest of your lives."

The monitor went dark.

Nova let out a shaky breath, realizing that she'd been holding her breath for three years. Being with Jacob was magical. She'd rather be on the run with Jacob than safe at home alone, so it was always worth it.

But she caught herself subconsciously looking at the crowds at the marketplace to make sure she didn't see a familiar or suspicious face. They never went to concerts or the theater, though Malta had a full and appealing cultural life. Their home had extraordinary security, but still she'd come awake with a pounding heart, adrenalin spiking, at the slightest sound in the night. They kept a go bag always packed with essentials, cash and jewels and several IDs. Just in case.

The possibility of imminent danger was always a low buzz in their heads, constantly.

It was all over. Constant buzz of danger, fear of strangers, the possibility of having to abandon their wonderful new life in an instant—all gone. Wiped out as if those dark clouds had never been.

Nova gave another sob, leaning toward Jacob. Her rock.

He opened his arms and she crawled onto his lap, sighing as she felt his strong arms going around her. A fortress of strength surrounding her. The tears dried up and she exhaled and inhaled, the first free breath in forever.

"God, Jacob."

His arms tightened. "I know."

Her head found its usual spot against his chest. Against her skin, she could feel his strong, steady heartbeat. Her own erratic heartbeat started slowing down.

His cheek rested against the top of her head.

"It's over. I can hardly believe it."

"I can." His voice was a deep rumble in his chest, almost felt more than heard. "Took long enough. I've been working toward this for a long time."

She'd closed her eyes to savor his warmth and strength but now her eyes popped open. She looked up. "What?"

He smiled down at her. That first period, in his underground lair like a modern-day Hades dragging Persephone down to him, he'd smiled maybe twice in the time they'd been together. And even those smiles, though real, looked pained. As if his face was not built for a smile.

These days he smiled all the time.

"Darling Nova. Do you honestly think I'd leave our safety—*your* safety—purely to chance? I've been working on this from the start. First, I had to find a suitably ruthless minor mobster. They are a dime a dozen, but I had to find someone smart and truly ambitious. I eased his way to power, feeding him money and information. He never knew where they came from but he used both very well. Then I started feeding him intel on Petrov's weaknesses. How lucrative his businesses were, but how badly he was managing them. How easy he'd be to take down. I gave our mobster info on Petrov's lieutenants, how to track them. It took a while, so long that I thought maybe I'd chosen badly, but I hadn't. He waited for the right moment, he struck precisely, and eliminated the entire gang. Perfect planning, perfect timing, perfect execution. I couldn't have done it better myself."

A laugh bubbled up. "You planned the whole thing!"

"Yes." The smile broadened. "Soup to nuts, as they say. And it worked. Took more time than I thought it would, but it worked."

There were no words. She couldn't find any words to express her joy, her relief. Though he knew. He knew her very well by this point.

But if she couldn't give him words, there was something else she could give him.

She lifted her mouth to his, to this man who was everything to her. She was brimming with emotions she couldn't express with words but could express with desire.

The kiss grew heated in an instant. Heated, then almost desperate. There was no one in the house and they couldn't be seen from the sea. The entire palazzo embraced them. Jacob's hands were almost clumsy in his haste as he tried to undo the tiny buttons of her long linen shift, finally, with a low growl, just ripping the dress down the front.

It had been a long time since their lovemaking had had that raw desperate edge. They were married, lived together, the sex was usually relaxed and long lasting.

Not now. Now it was as if they'd never made love before. They were starting a completely new life. There was no time for foreplay, no desire for lengthy kisses and caresses.

Nova wanted her husband inside her just as fast as was humanly possible. Her panties flew over her shoulder, her husband opened his pants, he positioned her and slid right in. They both blew out a breath. Nova tightened her arms as her husband started moving in her, hard and fast, too fast to last. But she was primed too, and they came together.

She slumped boneless against Jacob, panting. Complete, fulfilled. A future of this—sex, yes, but also meals and walks and laughter—stretched out before them. A lifetime. Together.

Nova straightened. He was still inside her, semi-erect. Her groin and his were wet with their juices. Something about that...

She'd gone off the pill for three months, on the advice of her doctor. They'd been taking precautions.

Oh, God. They hadn't taken precautions...

Nova reared back and looked in horror at Jacob.

He kissed her on the cheek. "My darling wife. I think we just made a baby."

She stared at him. The horror receded, replaced by a tiny glow inside her, like being touched by magic.

"I want a girl," Jacob ordered.

THE END

ALSO BY LISA MARIE RICE

Murphy's Law

Woman On The Run

Fatal Heat

A Fine Specimen

The Italian

Don't Think Twice

Port Of Paradise

Protector

Runaway

ABOUT THE AUTHOR

Lisa Marie Rice is eternally 30 years old and will never age. She is tall and willowy and beautiful. Men drop at her feet like ripe pears. She has won every major book prize in the world. She is a black belt with advanced degrees in archaeology, nuclear physics, and Tibetan literature. She is a concert pianist. Did I mention her Nobel Prize?

Of course, Lisa Marie Rice is a virtual woman and exists only at the keyboard when writing romance. She disappears when the monitor winks off.